THE SONG OF ROLAND

THE SONG
OF ROLAND

Translated, with an
Introduction, by W. S. Merwin

Notes, Glossary, and
Select Bibliography by
M. A. Clermont-Ferrand
UNIVERSITY OF ST. THOMAS

THE MODERN LIBRARY
NEW YORK

LIBRARY OF CONGRESS CATALOGING-IN-PUBLICATION DATA
Chanson de Roland. English
The song of Roland / translated, with an introduction, by W. S. Merwin. — 1st ed.
p.   cm.
ISBN 0-375-75711-2
1. Roland (Legendary character)—Romances. 2. Epic poetry, French—
Translations into
English. 3. Knights and knighthood—Poetry. I. Merwin, W. S.
(William Stanley), 1927–
II. Title.
PQ1521.E5 M413 2001
841'.1–dc21   00-048989

CONTENTS

Introduction

W. S. Merwin

Some time near the end of July, Charles (Charles the King, Charles the Emperor, Charles the Great, Charlemagne) turned his army north toward the Pyrenees and France. The year was 778. He was thirty-six years old and he was not used to failure, but even the royal chroniclers would have difficulty in trying to describe his ambitious summer campaign in Spain as though it had been a success.

It had not been hastily conceived. Suleiman, the Moorish governor of Barcelona, had visited Charles in the spring of 777 to urge him to cross the Pyrenees, and the request, and Charles' response to it, were both influenced by dynastic and religious promptings which had histories of their own.

Suleiman was a member of the Abassid dynasty, descended from an uncle of Mohammed. Earlier in the century the Abassids had overthrown the reigning Umayyad dynasty and assassinated every member of it except one, Abdur Rahman, who had escaped to Spain and established himself there as the Emir. Suleiman's hatred of Rahman was understandable, and it had already led him to seek and to obtain the protection of his Christian neighbor, King Pepin of France, Charles' father.

There were other reasons why Charles would have been sympathetic to Suleiman. He was himself a member of a young dynasty, a matter of subtle importance in a world governed to a great degree by tradition. And then, Abdur Rahman, as the last representative of the Umayyads, stood for the family which, half a century before, had commanded the great Moorish invasion of France. At that time the apparently invincible Umayyads had forced their way as far north as Tours before Charles' grandfather, Charles Martel, turned them back. It was the Umayyads whom Charles' father, Pepin, had fought and at last driven from France.

But doubtless none of these considerations would have impelled Charles to cross the Pyrenees if it had not been for a more powerful and obvious motive: his own ambition. In the first nine years of his reign he had conquered Aquitaine, beaten the Saxons and the Lombards, and become the official guardian of Christendom, whose boundaries he had extended to the north and east. An expedition into Spain would give him a chance to unify the different parts of his realm in a common effort, and incidentally to conquer the as yet unsubjected Basque provinces. Suleiman probably stressed the apparent fact that Rahman was a menace to Charles' southern frontier, and very possibly he would have told the French king that if he were to attack Rahman now he could not help succeeding, that the Abassids themselves were raising an army of Berbers to send against the Umayyad, and that the people of Spain were on the point of rebellion. The exact details of the embassage and the terms of the agreement that was reached are not known. But by Easter 778 Charles was in Poitou with an immense army recruited from every part of his kingdom: it included Goths, contingents from Septimania and Provence, Austrasians, Neustrians, Lombards, Burgundians, and Bavarians. After Easter he crossed the western end of the Pyrenees, through the Basque country, at the head of half his army. He sent the other half around the eastern end of the mountains. They were to meet before Saragossa.

Just what happened that summer was carefully obscured in the accounts and will never be known. Certainly there were no great triumphs. The Christian natives of Spain did not hasten to overthrow the tolerant Moorish rule and welcome the Franks; on the contrary, the Christians of the kingdom of Asturias preferred their own indepen-

dence to the presence of a foreign army however dear to the Pope. It
is also possible that they were in league with Rahman. At any rate, they
resisted the Franks. The Christian city of Pampelona refused entry to
Charles and had to be stormed; it was the only city in the entire campaign which was actually taken. The native rebellion against Rahman
never amounted to much, and Suleiman himself had a falling out with
his Moorish allies on the African continent. When the Frankish army
assembled before Saragossa the city defied it, despite Suleiman's
diplomatic efforts; it is not known how hard Charles tried to take it,
but he had no siege machinery, and he failed. By some time in July he
had received the formal surrender of a few cities—a gesture which
may have owed as much to his alliance with Suleiman as it did to his
own army—and he had gained some hostages, and little else. There is
no way of knowing just why he abandoned the campaign so early in
the summer. It is possible that he saw nothing to be gained by staying,
in the circumstances, and was simply cutting his losses. Supplies may
have run dangerously low. It is conceivable that the campaign had
turned out far worse than the accounts would lead us to suppose, and
that the army was in fact retreating. Even if that were so it cannot have
been a rushed or disorderly retreat: in August the army stopped at
Pampelona long enough to raze the walls of the city to punish the in-
habitants for their resistance, and no doubt to weaken the Spanish side
of the frontier. It has been suggested (by Fawtier) that if Charles had
not been in a hurry, for some reason, he would have paused long
enough to celebrate the important feast of the Dormition of the Vir-
gin on August 15. At any event he did not do so, but pushed on into the
Pyrenees.

What happened next is one of the great riddles.

In the earliest history of Charles' expedition, the one included in a
chronicle known as the *Annales Royales,* there is no reference to any military action whatever in the Pyrenees. All later writers on the subject
have agreed that the author had something of importance to be silent
about. Of such importance, in fact, that his immediate successors evi-
dently felt that mere silence would not serve to conceal it, and set
about explaining it. The original *Annales* were rewritten and expanded
roughly a quarter of a century after they were first compiled. It was

long thought that the rewriting was done by Charlemagne's biographer Einhard, and though it is now certain that the changes are not his, the second edition of the chronicle is still referred to as the *Annales dites d'Einhard*. In this work there is a brief and contradictory account of something which happened on the way back from Spain. The Basques, it says here, from positions at the tops of the mountains, attacked the rear guard and put the whole army in disorder; the Franks were caught at a disadvantage and did badly; most of the commanders of the different sections of the army were killed, and the enemy, helped by the nature of the terrain, managed to carry off the baggage and escape. There is a reference, too, to the bitterness of Charles' grief.

Then there is Einhard's own account. In the first place he is more ingenious than his predecessors at making it sound as though the Spanish campaign had been a success; then, having built up the picture, he sets against it the Pyrenean ambush on the way back as a relatively minor mishap. It was the treacherous Gascons, he says; they waited until the army was spread out in a long line in the gorges, and then they rushed down and threw the baggage train and the rear guard into confusion. There was a battle in the valley and the Franks were thrown back. The Gascons killed their opponents, the rear guard, to a man, seized the baggage, and scattered under cover of night. Their flight was made easier by their light armor and the nature of the terrain. And then Einhard says, "In this battle Egginhard the royal seneschal, Anselm the Count of the Palace, and Hruodland, the Warden of the Breton Marches, were killed, with very many others." It is one of the only two glimpses in history of the knight whose name would come to evoke one of the richest bodies of legend in the Middle Ages, and one of its greatest poems. The other is a coin, worn, but still displaying on one side the name *Carlus*, and on the reverse, *Rodlan*.

One final mention of the battle, by the chroniclers, is of interest. While the army was making its way back from Spain, Charlemagne's wife, in France, gave birth to a son, Louis, who would be his heir. Sixty years after the battle Louis' own biographer, a writer known as The Astronome, in speaking of it said that the names of those who fell in that action were so well known that there was no need to repeat them.

Of all the battles of the period, this one probably has excited most curiosity, and almost nothing about it is definitely known. It is not mere historical interest in the sources of the Roland story which still draws the speculation of scholars to what scanty evidence has come down to our times. In this case the theories of how the legend developed from the event are even more than usually dependent upon a notion of what the event was: a bitter but militarily unimportant misfortune, on the one hand, or one of the critical defeats of Charlemagne's reign, on the other.

Bedier, one of the great students of medieval literature in modern times and the editor of the Oxford text of *La Chanson de Roland,* propounded the theory of the development of the legend which was generally accepted for years. The battle, he believed, was a minor event which had been remembered in the area near the battlefield and had become a local legend; from those beginnings it had been retold and developed in monasteries and pilgrim sanctuaries along the route leading to Santiago de Compostella, in Spain; the route crossed the Pyrenees at Roncevaux—the Roncesvalles associated with the Roland story. Bedier, incidentally, was convinced that a number of the French *chansons de geste* developed in more or less the same way and may have been written by monks, or at least in collaboration with monks. With reference to the *Roland,* in particular, he cites the fact that the pass at Roncevaux was commended for admiration (complete with a monumental cross said to be Carolingian and other relics claiming descent from Roland and the battle) by the monks at Roncevaux in the twelfth century; he points out that one variant of the Roland legend is contained in a twelfth-century guide written for the benefit of pilgrims to Santiago de Compostella.

Bedier's theory was published just before World War I. It was subjected to criticism in the following decades by a number of scholars; one of the most interesting countertheories was put forward by Fawtier (*La Chanson de Roland*) in 1933. Fawtier analyzes the chroniclers' references to the battle and bases his conclusions, in great part, on the weaknesses in their accounts. The chroniclers, he insists, cannot have it both ways. Was it merely a massacre of the rear guard, or did it in fact involve the whole army and "throw it into disorder"? He poses some other interesting questions. Why, for instance, should the baggage train have been at the rear of the march, when it was usual to have it in the middle, especially in mountain country? Why should so many of the leaders of the different sections of the army have been in the rear guard (of course the legend itself, with its story of the Ganelon-Roland dispute, answers this one, but the legend in its final form came much later and a great part of it is concerned with the peculiar drama of this very situation). How many of these details, and how much of the picture of the lightning raid from the mountaintops may have been attempts to minimize and explain away a terrible defeat which had happened while Charles himself was in command?

In Fawtier's view, the battle, whether it took place at Roncevaux or elsewhere, was one of the great disasters of Charlemagne's career. The army, hurrying into the Pyrenees, was caught in a classical ambush: the van was blocked, the rear was then attacked, and the Franks had to fight their way forward, section by section, suffering losses so appalling that Charles never really managed to reassemble the survivors on the other side of the mountains, and instead set about hastily reorganizing the strong points in Aquitaine as though he expected further troubles from Spain. In fact the magnitude of the defeat was one of the things about the action which caught the popular imagination and contributed to the growth of the legend around the heroic figure of the doomed commander of the rear guard, Hruodland, Rodlan, Roland.

The legend may have grown in the region around Roncevaux, but it was elaborated in other parts of the kingdom too. By the late eleventh century, when the poem was written, it was possible for the poet to display, without fear of correction, an ignorance of the geography of Spain and, for that matter, of southern France, which indicates not only that he himself came from somewhere far from that part of the world, but also that the story and its heroes had long been familiar in places remote from the original battlefield. An audience at Roncevaux might just have been able to go along with the poet's assumption that Córdoba was near the hill city of Saragossa, which in turn was on the sea; it is unlikely that, even in the Middle Ages when simple experience was so meek an authority, they would have heard without a murmur that Narbonne and Bordeaux both lay on the same road north from Roncevaux. Furthermore, this shows a total ignorance of the Santiago pilgrim route and its monasteries, an interesting fact in view of the theory that the poem was composed in one of those places, on that route.

In Fawtier's opinion the story of the defeat was carried across France by its veterans, and in various localities, as it took on the character of legend through repetition, it was cast, in whole or in part, into the form of ballads. It is true that none of these survive, but then very little of the popular literature of the time has survived. The monks had nothing to do with the composition of *La Chanson de Roland* itself (although two other, later variants of the legend were composed by clerics). On the contrary, it was the legend, and perhaps the poem itself, which prompted the ecclesiastics at Roncevaux to exploit the pass as a pilgrim attraction—an enterprise which may have contributed to the poem's preservation.

There has been considerable controversy as to just when *La Chanson de Roland* was written. It must have been some time in the latter half of the eleventh century, but it is not possible to be much more definite than that. The poem apparently was already well known in 1096 when, at the Council of Clermont, Pope Urban II made use of it in his appeal to the chivalry of France to follow in the steps of Charlemagne and send an army against Islam. Many of the crusaders who responded to Urban's summons, and many who came later, must have been following an image of themselves which derived, at least in part, from the legendary last battle of the now transfigured Hruodland.

The poem, in its original form, has not survived. Modern knowledge of it is confined to six different versions, whose separate relations to the original are not plain. There is, for instance, a twelfth-century German translation by a Bavarian priest named Konrad. There is a Norse translation of the thirteenth century. There is a version in Franco-Italian, in the library of San Marco in Venice, which ends differently from the others. And there are three versions in French. One of them, known as *Recension O,* or the Oxford version, has survived in a single copy, Digby Mss 23, at the Bodleian Library, Oxford. It is supposed that it was a *jongleur's* copy of the poem. It is the oldest of all the versions, the most beautiful, and must have been much the closest to the original. Bedier's famous edition of the poem (the one I have used in making my translation) is based on the Oxford version, which Bedier compares at all points with the others.

Two other medieval retellings of the Roland legend are extant. One of them, the so-called *Pseudo-Turpin*, comes from Book IV of the twelfth-century *Guide to the Pilgrims of Santiago de Compostella*, to which I have already referred. It is in Latin prose and purports to have been written by the Archbishop Turpin himself. This worthy, as here presented, was with Charlemagne when Roland was attacked, and he had a vision in which he saw the soul of King Marsiliun being carried off by demons and the soul of Roland by angels. The narrative is clumsy, ill written, and encumbered with theological baggage. The other variant off the story, the *Carmen de prodicione Guenonis,* is also in Latin prose, but is shorter and more vigorous; it is possible that it is a translation of a lost French poem. A great deal of attention is paid to the character and actions of Ganelon. These two accounts, and the six surviving descendants of the *Chanson* itself, were compared by Gaston Paris, who concluded that the author of the *Pseudo-Turpin* knew the *Chanson* but that the author of the *Chanson* did not know the *Pseudo-Turpin* variant; that there was no evidence of any relationship between the *Pseudo-Turpin* and the *Carmen;* that there was no way of establishing any relationship between the *Carmen* and the *Chanson.*

No decision about the spelling of characters and places could have satisfied everyone, and between the two extremes of modernizing and Anglicizing everything, on the one hand, or of keeping to the medieval versions in every case, on the other, I have not even been consistent. It would have struck me as affected and pointlessly archaic to have insisted on the original versions of names which have become familiar in modern English—Roland, Charles, Ganelon, Reims, Bordeaux. The work, after all, is a translation to begin with. But with names which, in my judgment, had not acquired such familiarity, I have either followed one of the original versions (sometimes there are several: Marsile, Marsilies, Marsilie, Marsiliun, Naimun, Naimon, Neimes, Naimes) or Bedier's standardized modern French version (Blancandrin, Balaquer, Thierry, Seurin), depending on which seemed preferable in the circumstances.

The *Chanson de Roland*, as it has survived in the Oxford version, consists of just under 4000 lines, arranged in *laisses*, or groups of lines all ending on the same assonance. The metrical pattern is based on a ten-syllable line with a clear strong beat. There are several drawbacks to trying to reproduce anything of the kind in English. For one thing, the assonance patterns: English is far more meager than are the Romance languages in the number of similar assonances which can be found for any given word ending. There have been translations of *La Chanson de Roland* which have aimed at producing assonance patterns like those in the original, but the results have been gnarled, impacted, and stunted, as the original certainly is not. It would also have been possible—and this too has been done—to translate the poem into a ten-syllable line more or less resembling that of the original. The trouble is that the associations of the ten-syllable line in English are not at all what they are in French. It would have been very difficult not to invoke the tradition of iambic pentameter in English literature, a gallery of connotations which would not only have been irrelevant to the poem but which also could not help disguising it. This is quite apart from my own strong disposition against even reading another transposition of *La Chanson de Roland*, or most anything else, into a sort of blankish verse.

I am not questioning the splendor of the verse in the Oxford version, the magnificence of the noise it makes. It would be boorish of me to do so after the pleasure they have given me. But the qualities of the poem which finally claim me are all related to a certain limpidity not only in the language and the story but in the imagination behind them, to a clarity at once simple and formal, excited and cool, to characteristics which I find myself trying to describe in terms of light and water. These qualities obviously could not be reproduced in any translation but I wanted to suggest them, and it seemed to me that I should try to do it in prose.

———

W. S. MERWIN, recipient of the Pulitzer Prize and the PEN Translation Prize, is the author of more than fifteen books of poetry, most recently *The River Sound*, and numerous translations, including Dante's *Purgatorio*.

For Alice Lowell and Annella Brown

THE SONG OF ROLAND

THE SONG OF ROLAND

I

Charles the King, our great emperor, has stayed seven whole years in Spain and has conquered the haughty country as far as the sea. Not a single castle resists him any longer; not one wall has yet to be broken nor one city taken, except Saragossa, which is on a mountain and is held by King Marsiliun, who does not love God. Marsiliun serves Mahomet and prays to Appolin. But he cannot prevent harm from overtaking him.

II

King Marsiliun, in Saragossa, has gone out into the shade of an orchard. He reclines on a bench of blue marble. There are more than twenty thousand men around him. He summons his dukes and his counts: "Lords, hear this, regarding the scourge which has come upon us. The emperor Charles has come to this country from sweet France to destroy us. I have no host with which to offer him battle, nor such an army as could crush his. Give me counsel, my men of wisdom, to save me from death and shame!"

None of the pagans says a word in reply, except Blancandrin, from the Castle of Val-Fonde.

III

Blancandrin was one of the wisest of the pagans. He was well en-
dowed with the kind of courage which befits a knight, and he had
shrewdness and judgment to bring to the aid of his lord. And he said
to the King: "Do not give way to alarm! Send promises of faithful service and great friendship to Charles, the proud, the haughty. Send him
bears and lions and dogs, seven hundred camels and a thousand new-
molted falcons, four hundred mules weighed down with gold and silver, fifty wagons for him to range in a wagon train. He will be able to
pay his mercenaries well. Tell him that he has made war long enough
in this country, that he would do well to return to Aix, in France. Tell
him that you will meet him there at Michaelmas and bow to the law of
the Christians and become his vassal, in all honor and good faith. If he
demands hostages send him ten or twenty to gain his confidence. Let
us send the sons of our own wives. I will send my own son, even at the
risk of his life. It is far better that our children should lose their heads
than that we should forfeit our honor and possessions, or be reduced
to begging."

IV

Blancandrin said: "I will swear by this right hand, by this beard
which the wind flutters at my breast, that you will see the French
army break camp at once. The Franks will go back into France, to
their country. When each man has returned to the place which is
dearest to him, at Michaelmas Charles will hold high court in his
chapel at Aix. The day will arrive, the allotted time will run out, and
Charles will receive no word from us, no tidings. The King is proud,
and he has a hard heart. He will command them to take our hostages
and strike off their heads. It is far better that they should lose their
heads than that we should forfeit serene lovely Spain or endure suffering or distress!"

The pagans say: "Perhaps he is right."

V

King Marsiliun has brought his council to an end. He summons Clarin of Balaguet, Estamarin and his friend Eudropin, and Priamun and Guarlan the Bearded, and Machiner and his uncle Maheu, and Jouner, and Malbien from across the sea, and Blancandrin, to speak in his name. He calls to one side ten of the wiliest and most treacherous. "My lords, barons, you will go to Charlemagne. He is laying siege to the city of Cordres. You will approach him carrying olive branches in your hands to signify peace and humility. If you are cunning enough to arrange an agreement for me, I will give you as much gold and silver as you could wish for, and as much land, and as many possessions."

The pagans answer: "We are more than satisfied!"

VI

King Marsiliun has brought his council to an end. He says to his men: "Go, my lords. You will carry olive branches in your hands. In my name you will speak to King Charlemagne, asking him to have mercy on me in the name of his God. Tell him that he will not see the end of this first month before I have joined him with a thousand of my followers, and that I shall bow to the law of the Christians and become his vassal in all friendship and good faith. If he demands hostages he may have them."

Blancandrin says: "It will be to your advantage."

VII

Marsiliun commands his servants to lead out ten white mules which had been given to him by the King of Suatilie. The bits are made of gold, and the saddles are overlaid with silver. The messengers mount, bearing olive branches in their hands. They have come to Charles, who has France for his domain. They will deceive him to some extent; it cannot be helped.

VIII

The Emperor has become light-hearted and gay. He has taken Cordres and smashed its walls, and with his catapults he has battered down its towers. His knights have seized great quantities of plunder: gold and silver and rich garments. There is not a pagan left in the city: every one of them was either killed or became a Christian. The Emperor is in a broad orchard, and with him are Roland and Oliver, the Duke Sansun, and the proud Anseis, and Gefrey of Anjou, the King's standard-bearer. Gerin and Gerer are with them also, and many others. There are fifteen thousand from sweet France. The knights are seated on white silk carpets. The clever and the elderly are amusing themselves at backgammon and chess; the quick-blooded young men are fencing. Under a pine tree near an eglantine they have set a throne of pure gold, and there sits the King who rules sweet France. His beard is white and his hair is in full flower. His body is noble and his bearing is princely. If a man were to come looking for him, there would be no need to point him out. The messengers dismount and greet him, making protestations of friendship and good will.

IX

Blancandrin speaks before any of the others, and he says to the King: "Hail in the name of the glorious God whom we should adore! This is the message which the worthy King Marsiliun sends to you. He has inquired deeply into the law of salvation. He wishes to shower you with gifts chosen from among his own possessions: bears and lions, leashed boarhounds, seven hundred camels and a thousand falcons lately mewed, four hundred mules weighed down with gold and silver, fifty wagons to range in a wagon train, every one of them groaning with gold coin. You will be able to pay your mercenaries well. You have been in this country long enough. It would be better if you went back to Aix, in France. My lord promises that he will join you there."

The Emperor lifts up his hands to God, then he bows his head and begins to ponder.

X

The Emperor sits with head bowed. He was never hasty of speech. It is his custom to speak only in his own good time. When he raises his head his face is filled with pride. He says to the messengers: "You have spoken well. But King Marsiliun has proved that he is my enemy. What should make me put any confidence in this message which you bring?"

"Hostages," says the Saracen. "You may have ten, or fifteen, or twenty. I will send one of my own sons, even at the risk of his life, and I am certain that you will be given others who are yet better born than he. When you are in your royal palace, my lord promises that he will join you at the high feast of Saint Michael of Peril. And there, in the baths which were made for you by God himself, he will become a Christian."

Charles answers: "He may yet be saved."

XI

The evening was fair, the sun shone brightly. Charles commands his servants to stable the ten mules. He orders them to pitch a tent in the broad orchard, and he lodges the ten messengers there, sending twelve sergeants to wait upon them. There they have stayed through the night, until the coming of the bright day. The Emperor rises in the morning, hears mass and matins, and then goes under a pine and calls his barons together to council. He wants whatever he does to be in keeping with the advice of his Franks.

XII

The Emperor goes under a pine and calls his barons to council: Duke Oger and Archbishop Turpin, Richard the Elder and his nephew Henry, and Acelin the brave Count of Gascony, Tedbalt of Reims and his cousin Milun. Gerer and Gerin came too, and with them Roland, and the good, the noble Oliver. There were more than a thousand

Franks, come from France. And Ganelon came—the author of the betrayal. Then the council began which led to disaster.

XIII

Charles, the Emperor, speaks: "My lords, barons, King Marsiliun has sent his messengers to me. He wishes to present me with a splendid gift out of his own possessions: bears and lions, boarhounds which can be led on the leash, seven hundred camels and a thousand falcons for the mews, four hundred mules weighed down with gold from Arabia, and more than fifty wagons besides. But he asks me to return to France. He says he will join me at Aix in my palace, and will submit to our most holy law and become a Christian, and hold his lands under me as my vassal. But I cannot tell what he has in his heart."

The French say: "We must be on our guard."

XIV

The Emperor has ended his speech. Count Roland is not in favor of the proposal. He gets to his feet at once and comes forward to argue against it. He says to the King: "If you believe Marsiliun you will live to regret it. Here we have been for seven whole years in Spain, and I have conquered Noples and Commibles for you, and Valterne and the country of Pine, and Balasgued and Tuele and Sezilie. And King Marsiliun has already betrayed us. He sent fifteen of his pagans, each carrying an olive branch, and they all said these same words to you. And you did as your Franks suggested—they must have been lightheaded when they advised you. You sent two of your counts to the pagan, one of them was Basan and the other Basilie. He cut off their heads there in the mountains below Haltilie. Carry on with the war as you began it. Take the host which you have assembled and attack Saragossa and lay siege to the city. Let the struggle continue for the rest of your life, if necessary, but avenge those whom this villain murdered."

XV

The Emperor sits with his head bowed and strokes his beard and smooths his mustache. He neither agrees nor disagrees with his nephew; he does not answer him. None of the Franks says a word, except Ganelon. He gets to his feet and comes before Charles. He begins his speech in a haughty manner, saying:

"You will live to regret it if you lend your ear to some good-for-nothing, myself or another, who does not have your best interests at heart. When King Marsiliun sends to tell you that he is willing to clasp hands and become your vassal, when he offers to rule all of Spain through your gift and says that he will submit to our law, then whoever tells you that we should reject his offer, Sire, does not much care what kind of death we may die. It is not right that the promptings of arrogance should prevail. Let us ignore the fools and cleave to the wise!"

XVI

After this Naimes comes forward. There is not better vassal in the court. And he says to the King:

"You have heard Ganelon's answer. There is wisdom in what he says, if it is properly understood. King Marsiliun is beaten. You have taken all his castles, your catapults have smashed his walls, you have burned his cities and routed his followers. When he begs you to have mercy on him it would be a sin if you were to go on. Since he offers to give you hostages as security, this great war should not go any further."

The French say: "The Duke has spoken well."

XVII

"My lords, barons, who shall we send to King Marsiliun in Saragossa?"

The Duke of Naimes answers: "I will go, if you will send me. Give me the glove and the staff."

The King answers: "You are a wise man. And by this beard and by this mustache of mine you will not get so far from me so quickly. Go and sit down, since no one sent for you!"

XVIII

"My lords, barons, whom can we send to the Saracen who rules Saragossa?"

Roland answers: "Certainly I can go."

"Indeed you shall not go," Count Oliver says. "Your temper is rough and haughty. I am afraid you would start a quarrel. If the King wishes, I can certainly go."

The King replies: "Be still, both of you. Neither you nor he will move a step. By this white beard, I will curse any man who names one of the twelve peers!"

The French are silenced. They say nothing.

XIX

Turpin of Reims rises, comes from his rank, and says to the King:

"Let your Franks rest for a little while. You have been in this country for seven years and they have endured hardship and suffering. Give me the staff and glove, Sire, and I will go to the Saracen of Spain. I would be glad to see what he looks like."

The Emperor answers him in anger: "Go and sit down on that white carpet, and do not speak again unless I ask you!"

XX

"French knights," the Emperor Charles says, "Choose me a baron from my own country to carry my message to Marsiliun."

Roland says: "You could send my stepfather, Ganelon."

The French say: "Indeed, he could do it. If you do not send him you will not find anyone better."

And Count Ganelon is distraught. He throws off the great sable mantle from around his neck, and stands up in his silk shirt. His eyes are gray and his face is haughty; a noble carriage, a broad chest. He is so handsome that all the peers stare at him. He says to Roland:

"You great fool! What set you raving? I am your own stepfather, as everyone knows, and yet you single me out to be sent to Marsiliun. If God permits me to come back from there I will see to it that misfortune follows you for the rest of your life."

Roland answers: "Pride and foolishness! Everyone knows how little I care for threats. But since the messenger ought to be a man of sense, if the King will let me I will go in your place."

XXI

Ganelon answers: "You will do nothing of the kind! You are not my vassal nor am I your lord. It is Charles who commands me to perform this service, and I will go to Saragossa, to Marsiliun. But before this anger of mine is appeased I shall have played a trick of my own."

And at these words Roland laughs.

XXII

At the sight of Roland laughing, Ganelon is convulsed with rage. Beside himself with fury, he says to the Count:

"Do not think I have any love for you. You have settled this undeserved choice on me. Just Emperor, here I am before you. I wish to do your bidding."

XXIII

"I know that I am the one who must go to Saragossa, and whoever goes there will not come back. But above all remember that my wife is your sister, and that by her I have a son named Baldewin. No one is more handsome than he. He will make an excellent knight. I leave my lands and fiefs to him. Take good care of him. I shall not see him with these eyes again."

Charles answers: "You are too tender-hearted. I have given the command. You must go."

XXIV

The King says to Ganelon: "Come here before me and receive the staff and the glove. You have heard the Franks choose you."

Ganelon says: "Sire, it was Roland's doing. I will lose no love on him as long as I live, nor on Oliver either, for being his comrade. And here, Sire, before your eyes I defy the twelve peers because of the great love they bear him."

The King says: "Your anger exceeds all moderation. Now go, since I have given the command."

"I will go, and with no better prospect of safety than Basilie had, or his brother Basan."

XXV

The King holds out his right glove to Ganelon, but the Count is intent upon wishing that he were somewhere else, and when he puts out his hand to take it, it falls to the ground.

The French say: "Oh God, what can that mean? This embassage will bring disaster upon us."

"Lords," Ganelon says, "You may expect news!"

XXVI

"Sire," Ganelon says, "Give me your leave to depart. Since I must go, there is no use delaying."

"Go," the King says, "In Jesus' name and mine."

With his right hand he absolves the Count and makes the sign of the cross. Then he gives him the staff and the letter.

XXVII

Count Ganelon goes to his tent and begins his preparations, putting on his richest equipment, fastening gold spurs to his feet and girding his sword Murglies to his side. Then while his uncle Guinemer holds the stirrup, he mounts Tachebrun, his charger. There you would have seen many knights weeping, saying to him:

"We are grieved that this has befallen you! You have been in the King's court for a long time, and all have spoken of you as a noble vassal. Charlemagne himself cannot save or protect the man who chose you to go to Marsiliun. Count Roland should never have thought of suggesting you, who are descended from so exalted a lineage."

Then they say: "Sire, take us with you."

Ganelon answers: "No, in the name of God! It is better that I should die alone than that so many excellent knights should perish too. When you return to sweet France, my lords, greet my wife for me, and Pinabel my friend and comrade, and my son Baldewin, whom you know. Give him your allegiance and serve him faithfully."

He spurs into the path and sets out on his way.

XXVIII

Ganelon rides under a tall olive tree, and there he joins the Saracen messengers. Blancandrin reins in beside him, and the two converse with great cunning.

Blancandrin says: "Charles is a wonderful man. He has conquered Puille and the whole of Calabria, and crossed the salt sea into England, where he exacted tribute for Saint Peter. What does he want from us, here in our country?"

Ganelon answers: "Such is his nature. There was never a man to equal him."

XXIX

Blancandrin says: "The Franks are noble and admirable. But these dukes and counts bring great harm upon their lord, counseling him as they do. They waste his resources and they mislead him and others."

Ganelon answers: "That is true of no one, to my knowledge, except Roland, who will suffer shame for it one day. Yesterday morning when the Emperor was sitting in the shade, his nephew came up to him, wearing a mailed tunic, bringing him booty from Carcassonne. He held out a red apple in his hand.

" 'Take it, fair Sire,' Roland said to his uncle. 'I present you with the crowns of all kings.'

"His arrogance should be his undoing, for there is never a day when he does not risk death. If someone were to kill him we could live in peace."

XXX

Blancandrin says: "Roland is utterly evil. He wants to make all nations bow down to him. He wants to leave no country unchallenged. What people does he expect to help him in all this?"

Ganelon answers: "The French. They have such love for him that they would not willingly fail him in anything. He lavishes gold and silver on them, and mules, and war horses, and silks, and armor. Even the Emperor lets him have his way, for Roland will conquer countries for him from here to the Orient."

XXXI

They ride along together and in the end Ganelon and Blancandrin swear to each other that they will try to find some means of bringing about the death of Roland. They ride on down the roads and paths until they come to Saragossa and dismount under a yew tree. There, in the shadow of a pine, is a throne covered with Alexandrian silk. On it sits the King who rules over all of Spain. Around him are assembled twenty thousand Saracens, in absolute silence, waiting to hear the news.

Ganelon and Blancandrin arrive.

XXXII

Blancandrin, leading Count Ganelon by the fist, comes before Marsiliun and says to the King:

"Salutations in the name of Mahomet and in the name of Apollin, whose holy laws we keep. We have delivered your message to Charlemagne. He raised both his hands to heaven and gave praise to his God, and made us no other answer. Here he sends you one of his noble barons, a great man of France, from whom you will hear whether or not you will have peace."

Marsiliun answers: "Let him speak. We will listen."

XXXIII

Ganelon had laid his plans with care. Now he begins to speak, and he does it artfully, for he is skilled in the ways of eloquence. He says to the King:

"Salutations in the name of God, the Glorious, to whom we owe adoration. Here is the message which the worthy Charlemagne sends you. Receive the holy Christian faith and he will give you half of Spain as your fief. Refuse, and you will be taken by force and bound and transported to the city of Aix, where sentence will be pronounced upon your life and you will die a vile and shameful death."

King Marsiliun is filled with dread. He seizes a gold-fletched javelin and raises it, and nothing but the hand of one of his courtiers prevents him from hurling it.

XXXIV

King Marsiliun has turned pale. He brandishes the shaft of his javelin. At this sight Ganelon grasps his sword and draws it two finger lengths out of the sheath, and says to it:

"Oh fair bright blade which I have worn in the King's court all these years! The Emperor of France will never hear it said that I died alone in a strange country without your having made them pay some of their best blood."

The pagans say: "Let us not come to blows."

XXXV

The best of the Saracens have at last prevailed on Marsiliun to seat himself again on the throne. The Caliph says:

"You discredit us, offering to strike the Frank. You should lend him your attention, and listen."

"Sire," Ganelon says, "I have no choice but to suffer all this. But if I am allowed to speak, not all the gold that God made, nor all the riches of this country, will dissuade me from delivering the message which Charles, the mighty King, sends through me to his mortal enemy."

He is wearing a cloak of sable covered with Alexandrian silk. He flings it aside; Blancandrin catches it. But he keeps his sword, his right hand grasping the gold hilt.

The pagans say: "Here indeed is a noble baron!"

XXXVI

Ganelon approaches the King and says to him:

"You are wrong to be angry, for Charles, who rules France, sends to tell you that if you will receive the law of the Christians he will give you half of Spain in fief. The other half will go to his nephew Roland: you will certainly have an arrogant partner! If you reject this offer, Charles will advance on Saragossa and besiege you here, and you will be taken by force, bound, and without further ceremony brought to the city of Aix. You will have neither palfrey nor war horse, mule nor she-mule to ride on the way there. You will be thrown onto a wretched beast of burden, and when you arrive you will be sentenced and your head will be struck off. Our Emperor sends you this letter."

In his right hand he holds it out to the pagan.

XXXVII

Marsiliun, pale with anger, breaks the seal, flings the wax aside, looks at the letter and sees what is written there:

"Charles, who has France for his domain, bids me remember his grief and anger when I cut off the heads of Basan and his brother Basilie, in the mountains of Haltilie. Now if I wish to purchase my life I must send him my uncle the Caliph. Otherwise I need never hope for his favor."

Then Marsiliun's son speaks. He says to the King:

"Everything which Ganelon has uttered is foolishness. He has gone too far. He should not be allowed to live any longer. Give him to me. I will do justice upon him."

When Ganelon hears this he sets his back against the trunk of a pine tree and brandishes his sword.

XXXVIII

Marsiliun withdraws into the orchard, taking with him the best of his vassals. Gray-haired Blancandrin goes with him, and Jurfaret, the King's son and heir, and Marsiliun's uncle the Caliph and his followers.

Blancandrin says: "Call the Frenchman here. He swore to me that he would help us."

The King says: "Go yourself and bring him."

Blancandrin takes Ganelon by the hand and leads him from the dais into the orchard, to the King. There they plot the unpardonable betrayal.

XXXIX

"Fair sir, Ganelon," Marsiliun says to him, "in the heat of my anger I behaved somewhat rashly toward you, threatening to strike you as I did. I swear to you by these sable skins, whose gold mountings are worth more than five hundred pounds, that before tomorrow night you will have been given a handsome compensation."

Ganelon answers: "I shall not refuse it. May God be pleased to reward you for it."

XL

Marsiliun says: "Ganelon, the truth is that I should be happy to take you into my favor. Now tell me about Charlemagne. He is very old. He has outworn his time. To my certain knowledge he has been alive for over two hundred years. He has taken his body to so many countries, he has received so many blows on his shield, he has reduced so many rich kings to beggary—will he never grow tired of making war?"

Ganelon answers: "Charles is not as you suppose. Everyone who sees him and comes to know him agrees that the Emperor is a great man. It would be impossible for me to exaggerate his glory and his virtues, or to praise them too highly. His courage is beyond description. And God has kindled such nobility in him that he would rather die than fail his barons."

XLI

The pagan says, "I am filled with amazement, and I have good reason. Charlemagne is old and his beard is gray and his hair is white. To my certain knowledge he has been alive for two hundred years and more. He has dragged his body to so many lands, he has taken so many blows from lances and from spears, and he has reduced so many kings to begging—when will he be tired of making war?"

"Never," says Ganelon, "as long as his nephew is alive. There is not another vassal to compare with him under the hood of heaven. And his companion Oliver, too, is an excellent knight. And the twelve peers, whom Charles holds in such tender esteem, and twenty thousand knights with them, make up his vanguard. Charles is safe. He is not afraid of any man alive."

XLII

The Saracen says: "I am filled with astonishment at Charlemagne, with his gray and white locks. He has been alive, to my certain knowledge, for two hundred years and more. He has traveled through so many countries, conquering them, and he has taken so many blows from good sharp spears, and he has killed so many kings and overthrown them on the field—will he never grow tired of making war?"

"Never," Ganelon says, "as long as Roland is alive. There is not another vassal to compare with him from here to the Orient. And worthy Oliver, his companion, is another excellent knight. And the twelve peers, who are so precious to Charles, and twenty thousand knights with them, make up his vanguard. Charles is safe. He fears no man alive."

XLIII

"Fair sir, Ganelon," King Marsiliun says, "never will you see an army more splendid than mine. I can assemble four hundred thousand knights. Do I dare give battle to Charles and the French?"

Ganelon answers, "Do nothing of the kind, for the moment. You will lose great numbers of your pagans. Turn from folly and cleave to wisdom: out of your wealth present the Emperor with so rich a gift that all the French marvel at it. If you send him twenty hostages the King will return to sweet France. He will leave his rear guard behind. Unless I am wrong Count Roland his nephew will be there, and brave courtly Oliver, and if I can find someone who will listen to what I have to say, both of them will be killed. Charles will behold the downfall of his great pride, and he will have no heart for making war against you any more."

XLIV

"Fair sir, Ganelon, how can I kill Roland?"

Ganelon answers: "I can tell you that, without any doubt. The King will proceed to the main pass through the mountains, at Sizer, leaving his rear guard behind him, with his nephew Count Roland, and Oliver, in whom Roland places such trust. There will be twenty thousand Franks in their company. Send a hundred thousand of your pagans against them and engage them in a first battle. The French host will be battered and shaken, and I must tell you now that your own men will suffer great losses. But send the same number against them a second time and give them battle. Whether in the first onslaught or the second, Roland is sure to be killed, and you will have achieved a noble and knightly deed, and will be free of war for as long as you live."

XLV

"If anyone could bring about the death of Roland, Charles would have lost his own body's right arm. There would be no more of these awe-inspiring armies. Charles would never again assemble these great hosts, and France, the land of our sires, would be left in peace."

When Marsiliun hears this he kisses Ganelon on the neck, and then turns to where his treasures are kept.

XLVI

Marsiliun says: "Whatever we say, all our agreements are worthless unless you will swear to me to betray Roland."

Ganelon answers: "I will do as you wish." On the holy relics in his sword Murglies he swears to betray Roland, and so his treachery is sealed.

XLVII

There is an ivory throne there. Marsiliun sends for a book containing the laws of Mahomet and Termagant, and he, the Saracen of Spain, swears that if he finds Roland in the rear guard he will attack with his entire army and kill him if he can.

Ganelon answers: "May your wish be fulfilled!"

XLVIII

Then Valdabrun, a pagan, comes forward and approaches King Marsiliun. Laughing pleasantly, he says to Ganelon:

"Take this sword. No man has a better one. The hilt alone is worth more than a thousand of our gold pieces. Fair sir, I give it to you as a token of friendship, so that you will help us to deal with Roland: make sure that we are able to find this baron in the rear guard."

"It shall be done," Count Ganelon answers. Then they kiss each other's cheeks and chins.

XLIX

After that Climorin, a pagan, approaches and, laughing pleasantly, says to Ganelon:

"Take my helmet. I have never seen a better one. And lend us your help against this Roland, lord of the marches, so that we may bring him to shame."

"It shall be done," Ganelon answers. Then they kiss each other's mouths and faces.

L

Then Bramimunde, the Queen, approaches.

"Sir," she says to the Count, "my lord and all his men hold you high in their favor, and my love for you, accordingly, is great. I send your wife these two necklaces heavy with gold, amethysts and jacinths. They are worth more than all the riches of Rome. Your Emperor never owned any to compare with them."

He takes them and puts them into his pouch.

LI

The King summons Malduit, his treasurer: "Have you made ready the gifts which are to be sent to Charles?"

And he replies: "Yes, Sire, they are ready: seven hundred camels laden with gold and silver, and twenty hostages chosen from the noblest under heaven."

LII

Marsiliun takes Ganelon by the shoulder and says to him:

"You are very brave and very wise. In the name of that law which to you is most holy, do not withdraw your heart from us. I will lavish gifts on you out of my own possessions: ten mules laden with fine gold from Arabia. And not a year will pass but I will send you the same again. Here, take the keys of this wide city. Present these treasures to King Charles. Then arrange matters so that Roland is in the rear guard. If I can find him in any pass or ravine, I will attack and fight him to the death."

Ganelon answers: "I must not delay my return any longer."

Then he mounts and sets out on his way.

LIII

The Emperor, starting his homeward journey, comes to the city of Galne, which Count Roland had taken for him and destroyed. After the day of its overthrow the city was deserted for a hundred years. The

King waits for news of Ganelon, and for tribute from the great land of Spain. As dawn breaks and the day brightens Count Ganelon rides into the encampment.

LIV

The Emperor rises in the morning. The King hears mass and matins and then stands on the green grass before his tent. Roland is there, and brave Oliver, the Duke Naimes, and many of the others. Ganelon, the villain, the traitor, comes and begins a cunning speech, saying to the King:

"Salutations in the name of God! Here I bring you the keys of Saragossa, and all this treasure, and twenty hostages—let them be well guarded. And the brave King Marsiliun begs you not to blame him for failing to send you the Caliph, for with my own eyes I have seen four hundred thousand armed men, in their hauberks, and many of them with their helmets laced, wearing swords with hilts of carved gold, go with the Caliph and embark on the sea. They fled from Marsiliun rather than become Christians. Before they were four leagues out on the water, storm and tempest swallowed them up. They were drowned. You will never see any of them again. If the Caliph had been alive I would have brought him to you.

"As for the pagan king, Sire, you may be certain that you will not see this first month pass without his following you to the Kingdom of France, where he will bow to the law which you observe, and where with clasped hands he will become your vassal, to rule the Kingdom of Spain as your tributary."

The King says: "God be thanked. You have done well. You will be well rewarded."

At his command a thousand trumpets sound through that host. The Franks break camp, load their beasts of burden, and all set out on the road for sweet France.

LV

Charles the Great has ravaged Spain, seized its castles, sacked its cities. Now the King declares that his war is over. The Emperor rides toward sweet France.

Count Roland has fixed his pennon to his lance, and on the top of a mound he lifts it toward the sky. At this signal through all the surrounding country the Franks pitch camp.

Through the broad valleys the pagans ride, hauberks on, helmets laced, swords girded, their shields at their necks and their lances adorned with pennons. They halt in a wood high in the mountains, four hundred thousand of them, and wait for the dawn to break. Oh God, how terrible that the French know nothing of their presence!

LVI

The day passes, the night grows dark, and Charles, the mighty Emperor, sleeps. He dreams he is at the great gorges of the pass at Sizer, holding his ashen lance in his fist, and that Count Ganelon comes and seizes the lance and twists and shakes it so violently that the splinters fly toward heaven.

Charles sleeps on and does not wake.

LVII

After this vision he has another dream. He is in France, at Aix, in his chapel, and a fierce wild boar is biting his right arm. He sees a leopard come from the side toward the Ardenne, and savagely attack his body. Within the hall itself a boarhound descends, bounds toward Charles at a full run, tears the right ear from the first beast, and in a great rage attacks the leopard. The French declare it a marvelous combat and wonder which of the two will win.

Charles does not wake but sleeps on.

LVIII

The night passes and when the bright dawn appears the Emperor rides proudly through that host.

"My lords, barons," the Emperor Charles says, "you see before us the passes and narrow gorges. Who shall remain here in the rear guard?"

Ganelon answers: "Roland, my stepson. You have no braver vassal."

When the King hears this he stares hard and coldly at Ganelon and says to him: "You are a devil incarnate! Some deadly passion possesses your body. And who, then, should go before me in the vanguard?"

Ganelon answers: "Oger of Denmark. No baron of yours could better perform that service."

LIX

When Count Roland hears himself named he speaks as becomes a knight:

"Stepfather, my lord, my debt of affection to you is greater than ever, now that you have named me to the rear guard. I assure you that Charles, the King who rules France, will lose neither palfrey nor war horse, nor saddle mule, male or female, nor draft horse nor pack horse that has not first been bargained for with swords."

Ganelon answers: "I know what you say is true."

LX

When Roland hears that he will be in the rear guard he turns to his stepfather in anger and says:

"Ah, slave and coward, malicious heir of dishonored ancestors, did you think I would let the glove fall to the ground as you did the staff when you stood before Charles?"

LXI

"Just Emperor," says Roland, the baron, "give me the bow which you are holding in your fist. I am sure that no man will be able to reproach me with having dropped it, as Ganelon dropped the staff when he reached out his right hand to take it."

The Emperor's head is bowed. His hands drag at his beard and twist his mustache. He cannot keep the tears from flowing down his face.

LXII

After that Naimes comes forward. There is no finer vassal in the entire court. And he says to the King:

"You have heard how matters stand. Count Roland is in a fury. He has been named for the rear guard and no baron of yours can change that now. Give him the bow which you have bent and find him those companions who will be of most help to him."

The King holds it out and Roland takes it.

LXIII

The Emperor speaks to his nephew Roland.

"Fair sir, nephew, listen to my decision. I will make you a present of half of my army. Keep them with you and you will be safe."

To this the Count replies: "I will do no such thing. God confound me if I shame my ancestors! I will keep with me twenty thousand Franks noted for their bravery. And you may go on your way through the pass in utter confidence, and fear no man as long as I am alive."

LXIV

Count Roland has mounted his charger. His companion Oliver comes to join him. And Gerin and the brave Count Gerer also come to join him, and Otun and Berenger come to join him, and Astor and old Anseis come to join him, and the proud Gerard of Roussillon comes to join him, and the rich Duke Gaifer comes to join him.

The Archbishop says: "My head upon it, I am with you!"

"And I along with you," says Count Gualter. "I am Roland's vassal. I must not fail him."

Then among them they choose twenty thousand knights.

LXV

Count Roland summons Gualter of Hum.

"Take a thousand Franks from our land of France and hold the defiles and the heights so that the Emperor may not lose a single man."

Gualter answers: "I will do as you bid me."

Along the defiles and on the heights Gualter has ranged a thousand French from their land of France. However bad the news he will not descend from his positions before seven hundred swords have been unsheathed. Before that terrible day is over King Almaris from the kingdom of Belferne will launch a battle against him.

LXVI

The peaks are high and the valleys are dark, the gorges awesome under dun rocks. That day the French proceed sorrowfully through the pass. The sound of them can be heard fifteen leagues away. And they emerge at last in the land of their fathers and see Gascony, the domain of their lord, and then they remember their fiefs and honors, and girls and noble wives, and there is not one of them who is not so filled with pity that he weeps.

But more than any of the others Charles is racked with anguish because he has left his nephew in the gorges of Spain. Pity overcomes him. He weeps and cannot help it.

LXVII

The twelve peers have stayed behind in Spain, and twenty thousand Franks with them, fearless to a man and with no dread of death.

The Emperor returns into France, hiding his sorrowful face in his mantle. Duke Naimes rides beside him and says to the King:

"What is the cause of your grief?"

Charles answers: "It is wrong of any man to ask me! My sorrow is so great that I cannot bear it in silence. Ganelon will be the destruction of France. Last night an angel sent me a vision in which I saw Ganelon shatter my lance from between my fists. And he has named my nephew for the rear guard, and I have left Roland beyond the frontier in a foreign country. Oh God, if I lose him no one will take his place for me!"

LXVIII

Charles the Great weeps and cannot help it. At the sight of him a hundred thousand Franks are filled with tenderness and with an unreasoning fear for Roland. The villain Ganelon has betrayed him, and has accepted rich gifts from the pagan king: gold and silver, mantles and silks, mules, horses, camels and lions.

From all of Spain Marsiliun has summoned his barons, his counts, viscounts, dukes and commanders, his emirs, and the sons of the nobility. He has assembled four hundred thousand of them in three days. He gives orders to sound the drums in Saragossa. On the highest of the towers they raise an image of Mahomet, and every one of the pagans prays to it and worships it. Then they file out and ride with all possible speed through the land of Certeine, down the valleys and across the mountains, until they can see the pennons of the French. The rear guard under the twelve companions will not fail to offer them battle.

LXIX

Marsiliun's nephew comes forward, riding a mule which he urges along with a staff. His manner is pleasing, and with a laugh he says to his uncle:

"Fair Sire, King, I have served you long and have known suffering and hardship, and battles fought and won on the field. Grant me one favor: the first blow at Roland. I will kill him with my sharp spear. If Mahomet will protect me, I will strike off the fetters from the whole of Spain, from the Spanish passes all the way to Durestant. Charles will lose heart. The Franks will yield. You will have no more war as long as you live."

King Marsiliun has given him the glove.

LXX

Marsiliun's nephew holds the glove in his fist and addresses proud words to his uncle:

"Fair Sire, King, you have accorded me a great gift. Choose twelve of your barons to ride with me and give battle to the twelve companions."

Before any of the others have spoken, Fulsarun, the brother of King Marsiliun, answers:

"Fair Sire, nephew, you and I will go together against the rear guard of Charles' great host, and indeed we will give them their battle. It is decided: we will be the death of them."

LXXI

From another side King Corsalis comes forward. He is a native of Barbary, an adept of the black arts. He speaks like a true vassal. Not for all the gold of God, he says, would he be a coward.　．　．　．　．　．　．

．　．　．　．　．　．　．　．　．　．　．　．　．　．　．　．　．　．　．　．

Look now: Malprimis of Brigant spurs forward, who on foot can run faster than a horse. Before Marsiliun he calls out at the top of his voice:

"I will take my body to Roncesvalles. If I come upon Roland I will know how to dispatch him."

LXXII

There is in that company an Emir from Balasquez whose body is noble and handsome, and whose face is bold and open. When he is mounted on his horse he carries his arms proudly. He is renowned for his courage. If only he were a Christian he would be an excellent knight. He comes before Marsiliun and shouts:

"I will go and risk my body at Roncesvalles. If I find Roland he will meet his death then and there, and the same is true of Oliver and the twelve peers. The French will perish in sorrow and shame. Charles the Great is an old man in his dotage, and will have no more stomach for waging war. And Spain will be free, and will be left to us."

King Marsiliun has thanked him profusely.

LXXIII

There is in that company a commander from Moriane, and there is no greater villain in the land of Spain. He has made his boast before Marsiliun:

"I will lead my company to Roncesvalles: we are twenty thousand with shields and lances. If I find Roland I swear I will kill him and never a day will pass but Charles will grieve."

LXXIV

From another direction comes Turgis of Turteluse, a count; the whole city whose name he bears belongs to him. He nurses a deep hatred of Christians, and in the presence of Marsiliun he joins the others, saying to the King:

"Have no fear. Mahomet is worth more than Saint Peter of Rome.

Serve him and the field and its honors are ours. I will go to Roncesvalles and meet Roland and no man will be able to save him from death. Look: here is my sword. It is a good sword; it is long. I will measure it against Durendal and you will hear soon enough which one overtopped the other. The French will die if they venture against us, and Charles the Old will suffer grief and shame, and never wear crown again on this earth."

LXXV

From the opposite side comes Escremiz of Valterne, a Saracen, and lord of the land whose name he bears. From among all those who are assembled before Marsiliun, he shouts:

"I will go to Roncesvalles to bring pride to destruction. If I find Roland he will not bear away his head, nor will Oliver, who commands the others. The twelve peers are doomed, all of them. The French will die, France will be ruined, Charles will lack for good vassals."

LXXVI

From another direction comes Esturgant, a pagan, and with him Estramariz, one of his companions, villains both of them, and deceitful and treacherous. Marsiliun says to them:

"Approach, my lords! You will go to the gorges of the pass at Roncesvalles and lend your help in conducting my troops."

And they answer: "We will do as you command. We will attack Oliver and Roland, and nothing will save the twelve peers from death. We have good swords, they are sharp, they will run red with warm blood, the French will die, sorrow will settle upon Charles, we will give you the land of their fathers as a present. Come with us, King. You will see. It is true. We will give you the Emperor himself as a present."

LXXVII

Margarit of Seville, who rules over lands as far as Cazmarine, comes on the run. Because of his beauty he is a favorite with the ladies: there is not one of them who does not brighten and laugh with pleasure at the sight of him. No pagan is so excellent a knight. He enters the crowd before the throne and shouts to the King above all the others, saying:

"Have no fear! I will go to Roncesvalles to kill Roland, and Oliver will not bear away his life. The twelve peers are set aside for slaughter. Look: here is my sword. Its hilt is made of gold. It was a gift of an Emir of Primes. I promise you that it will be bathed in crimson blood. The French will die, France will be brought to shame, Charles the Old, with his beard in full flower, will know sorrow and rage every day for the rest of his life. Before a year is over we will have seized France and will be able to take our ease in the town of Saint-Denis."

The pagan king bows low to him.

LXXVIII

Chernuble of Munigre comes from the other side. His flowing hair reaches to the ground. When he is feeling playful he is able to lift and carry weights, merely in sport, that are heavier than the packloads of four sumpter mules. It is said that in the country from which he comes the sun does not shine, the wheat cannot grow, the rain does not fall, dew never forms, and all the stones are black. Some say that the land is inhabited by devils. Chernuble says:

"I have girded on my good sword, and I will dye it crimson at Roncesvalles. If I find the bold Roland in my path and do not attack him, never believe me again. I will strike down Durendal with my own blade. The French will die and France will be ruined."

When he has spoken, the twelve pagan peers assemble, and with them a hundred thousand Saracens, eager and impatient for battle. They go into a grove of pines and arm themselves.

LXXIX

The pagans arm themselves in Saracen hauberks, most of them made of three thicknesses of chain mail. They lace their fine Saragossa helmets. They gird on their swords made of steel from Viana. They carry resplendent shields and Valencian lances with white and blue and crimson pennons. They leave behind their saddle mules and palfreys and mount their war horses and ride in closed ranks.

The day was clear and the sun was fair. The light flashed from every piece of armor. A thousand trumpets are sounded, to add to the splendor. The din is tremendous, and it reaches the ears of the French. Oliver says:

"Sir, my companion, I believe the Saracens intend to do battle with us."

Roland answers: "Pray God that it may be so! For the sake of our king we are bound to remain here. For the sake of his lord a man is bound to suffer hardship, to endure the extremes of heat and of cold, and to lose, if he must, both hair and hide. Now let every man see to it that the blows he deals are heavy, lest a shameful song be sung of us. The pagans are in the wrong and the Christians in the right. No one will ever be able to say of me that I set a bad example."

LXXX

Oliver has climbed a peak, and looking to his right along a grassy valley, he sees the pagan host approaching. He calls to his companion Roland:

"From the side that is toward Spain there is a great noise coming, and I see approaching us so many bright hauberks, so many flashing helmets—they will bring bitter suffering to our Franks. Ganelon knew of this, that villain, that traitor, when he stood before the Emperor and named us for the rear guard."

"Silence, Oliver," Count Roland answers. "He is my stepfather. I will not have you say a word against him."

LXXXI

Oliver has climbed out of the heights, and from it he can see all the way into the kingdom of Spain, and he can see the enormous host of the Saracens. Their helmets are shining, studded with jewels set in gold; and their shields and their gilt-varnished hauberks are shining, and their lances and the pennons that are fastened to them. It is not possible to count even the separate companies of that host; the battalions are past numbering, there are so many. Oliver is greatly troubled at the sight. As fast as his horse will carry him he rides down from the peak and returns to the French and tells them what he has seen.

LXXXII

Oliver says: "I have seen the pagans. No man on earth ever saw more. In the vanguard are a hundred thousand with their shields ready, their helmets laced, their limbs in shining hauberks, the shafts of their lances raised and the burnished spears gleaming. You will have such a battle as was never seen before. Lords of France, God give you strength! Hold the field, let us not be beaten!"

The French say: "A curse on the man who runs away! Until death itself not one of us will fail you."

LXXXIII

Oliver says: "The pagans have a huge army, and our French appear to be very few. Therefore Roland, my companion, sound a blast on your horn. Charles will hear it, and he will return with his host."

Roland answers: "That would be the act of a fool! I would forfeit the fame I have in sweet France. Soon I will be striking great blows with my sword Durendal, and blood will cover the blade up as far as the hilt. These villainous pagans will suffer for coming to this gateway through the mountains. I promise you, they are all marked out for death."

LXXXIV

"Roland, my companion, sound your ivory horn, and Charles will hear it and command the army to return, and the King will come to our help with all his barons."

Roland answers: "God forbid that my ancestry should be shamed by an act of mine, or that I should make sweet France an object of scorn! Instead I will attack unsparingly with my good sword Durendal, which I have girded on here at my side. You will see this weapon running with blood from one end to the other. These villainous pagans will suffer for massing against us. I promise you, they are all marked out for destruction."

LXXXV

"Roland, my companion, sound a blast on your ivory horn. Charles will hear it as he marches through the pass, and I promise you the Franks will return."

Roland answers: "God forbid that any man living should be able to say that because of the pagans I blew my ivory horn! No one will ever be able to shame my family with the mention of such a thing. When I have joined in the massed battle I will strike a thousand blows and follow them with seven hundred more, and you will see the steel of Durendal running with blood. The French are brave, they will fight hard and well, and those who have come from Spain will not be saved from death."

LXXXVI

Oliver says: "I see nothing shameful in your sounding a blast now on your horn. I have seen the Saracens of Spain. The valley is covered with them, and the mountains, and the hills, and the plains. The foreigners have an enormous army, and there are few, very few, in our company."

Roland answers: "That makes me still more eager for battle. May

God in heaven and his angels forbid that the fame of France should be diminished because of me! I would rather die than be brought to shame. The Emperor's love will go to those who strike hardest."

LXXXVII

Roland is bold, and Oliver is wise. Both of them are renowned for their bravery. When they are armed and mounted no fear of death ever made them shrink from a battle. They are men of worth, these counts, and they speak proud words.

The villainous pagans ride on in great fury.

Oliver says: "Roland, now you can see a few of them. And they are near us, and Charles is far away. You would not deign to sound a blast on your ivory horn. If the King were here we would come to no harm. Look up along the pass that rises out of Spain, to the rear guard. You can see the sadness in their faces. Those who fight in this battle will never fight in another."

Roland answers: "No more of that vile talk! A curse on the heart which turns coward in its breast now! We will stay where we are, in our place. We will keep the field. And we will meet them with swinging swords and with blows of weapons."

LXXXVIII

When Roland sees that there will be a battle, his pride surpasses that of any lion or leopard. He calls out to the French and to Oliver:

"Sir, my companion, my friend, do not say such things! The Emperor set aside a full twenty thousand of his Franks to leave behind with us, and he knew that not one of them was a coward. For the sake of his lord a man must be prepared to suffer great hardships and to endure extreme cold and great heat. For the sake of his lord a man must be prepared to sacrifice even his blood and his flesh. Strike with your lance! And I will attack with my good sword Durendal, which the King gave me. And if I die, whoever takes it then will be able to say, 'It belonged to a noble knight.' "

LXXXIX

From another side Archbishop Turpin spurs his horse up a little hill, and there he raises his voice to preach a sermon to the French:

"Barons, my lords, Charles has left us here and if need be we must die for our King and to uphold Christendom! None of you can doubt that there will be a battle: now you can see the Saracens before you. Confess your sins and call upon God for his mercy, and for the salvation of your souls I shall grant you absolution. If you die, you will be holy martyrs and will sit in the topmost parts of Paradise."

The French dismount and kneel on the ground and the Archbishop blesses them in the name of God, and as a penance he bids them strike hard.

XC

The French straighten and rise to their feet, absolved and freed of their sins, and the Archbishop blesses them in the name of God. Then, armed according to the prescriptions of knighthood, and armored for battle from head to foot, they mount their chargers. Count Roland calls out to Oliver:

"Sir, my companion, you were right when you said that Ganelon had betrayed us all. He has received gold and possessions and money for his treachery, and may the Emperor take vengeance upon him on our account. King Marsiliun has bargained for our lives, but he will require swords when it comes to collecting his purchase."

XCI

Where the pass leads up out of Spain Roland has mounted Veillantif, his good swift horse. He has taken up his arms; his armor becomes him. Now with a flourish Roland the bold raises the point of his lance to heaven. Laced to the shaft is a white pennon whose fringes sweep down to his hands. He bears himself nobly; his countenance is candid and smiling. Behind him comes his companion, and the French, who regard him as their salvation. He turns and looks fiercely at the Saracens, and then humbly and sweetly at the French, whom he addresses courteously:

"My lords, barons, gently, and reined in to a walk, advance. These pagans are rushing upon their own destruction. Before nightfall we shall have seized spoils so rich and magnificent as to surpass in splendor any that were ever taken by a king of France."

At these words the two armies come together.

XCII

Oliver says: "I have no heart for talk. You would not deign to sound a blast on your ivory horn, and if you do not have Charles here at your side it is no fault of his, for that brave king knows nothing of what is happening here. And these knights who have stayed with us are blameless, whatever happens. Well then, let us ride with all our might against these Saracens. My lords, barons, keep the field! In the name of God I pray you, let every man resolve to strike hard and return blow for blow! Now let us not forget Charles' battle cry!"

At his words the French raise the battle cry "Mountjoy," and no man who had heard them could ever have forgotten the brave sound. Then—and oh God how fiercely—they charge. They spur their horses on faster and faster, and attack—what else could they do? And the Saracens receive their charge without flinching. Now the Franks and the pagans have come together.

XCIII

Marsiliun's nephew Aelroth is the first to ride out in front of the Saracen host and taunt our French with vicious words:

"Villainous French, today you will have a battle with us! You have been betrayed by him whose duty it was to protect you, and the king who left you here in the pass is a fool. Today France will be shorn of her fame, and Charles the Great will lose his body's right arm."

When Roland hears this, oh God what a rage fills him! He sets spur to his horse, lets it out to its best speed, and rides to hurl against the Saracen count the full fury of his attack. He smashes the shield, bursts apart the hauberk, rips up the breast, crushes the bones, forces the whole backbone out through the back, and with his spear drives out the soul. He spits the Saracen on his lance, and hoisting the body into the air, flings the corpse a spear's length from its horse, and the neck splits into two pieces. And still he does not leave it but addresses it in these words:

"Low wretch! Charles is no fool, and no lover of treachery! It was the act of a brave man to leave us at the pass, and France will lose none of her glory today. Now strike, Franks; let the first blows be ours! The right is with us, and this rabble is in the wrong."

XCIV

There is in that company a duke named Fulsarun, a brother of King Marsiliun's, who rules over the land of Dathan and Abiron. There is not a bloodier villain under heaven. His forehead, between his eyes, is enormous: if a man were to measure it it would prove to be over half a foot wide. At the sight of his nephew's death he is filled with grief and rides forward out of the ranks to offer combat to any who will fight with him; as he does so he shouts the pagan battle cry and flings a sharp taunt at the French:

"This very day sweet France will be shorn of her glory!"

Oliver hears him and is seized with anger. He claps his gilded spurs to his horse and like a true knight rides to fight with him. He breaks the shield, tears through the hauberk, drives lance, pennon, and all, into the body, and hurls the corpse a full spear's length out of the saddle. He looks down at the villain lying on the ground and makes him a proud speech:

"Low wretch, so much for your threats. Now strike, Franks, for they are surely ours!" And they shout, "Mountjoy!" which is Charles' battle cry.

XCV

There is in that company a king named Corsablis, from Barbary, that remote country. He calls out to the other Saracens:

"Surely we can win this battle, for there are so few of the French that we would be wrong not to hold them in contempt. Not one of them will Charles be able to save. The day of their death is here."

Archbishop Turpin hears every word and at once hates him worse than any man under heaven. He sets his spurs of fine gold to his horse and rides out bravely against him, breaks the shield, plows through the hauberk, drives his great lance into the body, skewers it, heaves it up, dead, and pitches the corpse onto the path a spear's length away. He turns and looks back at the villain on the ground. He will not leave him without addressing him, and he says:

"Pagan wretch, you lied! Charles, my lord, is our protector still, and our French have no wish to flee. We will leave your companions, every one of them, stalled in their places. Now learn this: death is your portion. Strike, Franks! Remember who you are! Give thanks to God: this first blow is ours!"

They raise the shout of "Mountjoy!" resolved to keep the field.

XCVI

And Gerin charges against Malprimis of Brigal, whose good shield, upon the impact, is not worth a farthing to him. Its crystal boss shatters; half of it falls to the ground. With his good lance Gerin rips through the hauberk into the flesh, spits the body; the pagan falls to the ground, a dead weight, and Satan carries off his soul.

XCVII

And his companion Gerer charges against the Emir, breaks his shield and parts the hauberk. His good lance drives on into the entrails, digs deep, passes clear through the body, and he leaves the corpse on the field a good spear's length away.

Oliver says: "We are fighting nobly!"

XCVIII

Duke Sansun rides to attack the Saracen general, breaks his shield which is gilded and painted with flowers, and his good hauberk protects him no better, but the spear splits heart, liver and lungs and leaves a corpse, whether any man mourns it or not.

The Archbishop says: "That was a stroke worthy of a knight!"

XCIX

And Anseis gives rein to his horse and rides to attack Turgis of Turteluse. He breaks his shield under the gilded boss, plows through his double hauberk, buries the head of his lance in the Saracen's body, drives it in deeper and out through the back, and tips the dead body into the field a good spear's length away.

Roland says: "That was a stroke worthy of a brave man!"

C

And Engeler, the Gascon from Bordeaux, sets spur to his horse, slackens the reins, rides out to attack Escremiz of Valterne, breaks the shield at his neck so that the pieces fly apart, smashes through the hood of his hauberk and into the throat between the collarbones. He knocks the corpse a good spear's length from the saddle, and then says to it:

"Now Hell has swallowed you up!"

CI

And Otun attacks a pagan by the name of Estorgans, strikes the leather cover of his shield and rips the crimson and white blazon into shreds, breaks through the skirt of his hauberk, runs his good sharp spear through the body and hurls the corpse from its swift horse. Then he says to it:

"Now nothing can save you!"

CII

And Berenger attacks Estramariz, breaks his shield, plows through his hauberk, runs his strong spear through the body and flings down the corpse in the middle of a thousand Saracens. Ten of the twelve pagan champions have been killed, and only two, Chernuble and Count Margarit, are still alive.

CIII

Margarit is a brave knight, handsome and strong, agile and nimble. He sets spur to his horse and charges against Oliver, breaks his shield under the golden boss, and drives the spear close to Oliver's side. But God preserves Oliver so that his body is not touched. The spear shaft breaks; Oliver keeps his saddle, and Margarit passes on, unchecked, and sounds his horn to rally his followers.

CIV

The battle becomes general, and magnificent. Count Roland does not spare himself; he fights with his spear as long as the shaft lasts, but after the fifteenth stroke it shatters and becomes useless. Then he draws his good sword Durendal, he bares the blade, and spurs his horse and charges against Chernuble. He cleaves the helmet glittering with carbuncles, sheers through the steel hood and leather coif, splits the skull and face between the eyes, and carving down through the polished hauberk made of fine mail, halves the whole body all the way to the groin. His sword plunges on, and passing through the saddle covered with beaten gold, sinks into the horse, severs its spine, grinding through no joint but through solid bone, and Roland hurls down horse and man, dead, on the rich grass of the meadow. Then he says to the corpse: "Wretch, you came here to your sorrow, and you will have no help now from Mahomet! It is not by such scum as you that a battle is won, and won quickly."

CV

Count Roland rides over the field, with Durendal, that good carver and cleaver, in his hand, and he wreaks carnage among the Saracens. You would have seen him fling corpse upon corpse, and the clear blood cascading into pools. His hauberk and both his arms, and the neck and shoulders of his horse, are covered with blood.

And Oliver fights on without resting. And the twelve peers deserve no reproach. And the French fight hard and furiously. There are pagans killed and others who grow faint. And the Archbishop says:

"A blessing upon our knights!"

And he cries, "Mountjoy!" which is Charles' battle cry.

CVI

And Oliver rides through the battle, with his spear shattered to a stump, charges against Malun, a pagan, breaks his gilded shield with the flowers painted on it, knocks the eyes out of his head and brings his brains tumbling down to his feet. He throws down the corpse among seven hundred other dead pagans, and turns and kills Turgis and Esturguz. But then even the stump of his spear snaps, and splits all the way down to his fist.

Roland says to him: "My companion, what are you doing? In a battle of this kind a club is not to my taste. Only iron and steel are worth anything. Where is your sword Halteclere with its guard of gold and its crystal pommel?"

"I have not had time to draw it," Oliver answers. "I have been too occupied with fighting."

CVII

Sir Oliver has drawn his sword at the urgent promptings of his companion Roland, and he displays its uses in knightly fashion. He attacks Justin of Val Ferree, a pagan, splits the whole of his head in two, cleaves the body, the gilt-varnished coat of mail, and the good saddle studded with jewels set in gold, severs the horse's spine, and hurls down onto the meadow before him the corpses of horse and rider.

Roland says: "Now I recognize you, brother! It is for blows like that one that the Emperor loves us."

And on all sides the shout of "Mountjoy!" goes up.

CVIII

Count Gerin, mounted on his horse Sorel, and his companion Gerer, on Passecerf, slacken their reins, dig in their spurs, and charge against a pagan named Timozel. One strikes his shield, the other his hauberk; both of their spears break off in his body, and they tip his corpse out of the saddle and leave it in a furrow. I have not heard it said, and I do not remember which of those two was swifter and more nimble.

And then Esprieris was killed by Engeler of Bordeaux.

And the Archbishop kills Siglorel for them, a magician who had already descended once into Hell, guided by Jupiter, whom he had compelled to the task by means of enchantments. Turpin says:

"He was marked out to be our victim."

Roland answers: "The wretch is finished. Brother Oliver, such blows as that one are a delight to see!"

CIX

The battle grows still more furious, with Frank and pagan giving and receiving tremendous blows, some attacking and others defending themselves. There are so many spears shattered and bloodied, so many pennons torn, and so many battle flags, so many good French cut down in their youth, who will never see their mothers nor their wives again, nor the Franks who are waiting for them in the pass!

Charles the Great weeps, he laments, but what good will that do? There will be no help for the rear guard. Ganelon did them a bad turn, that day when he went to Saragossa and sold his own vassals. And for that he will lose his life and his limbs. In the court at Aix he will be sentenced to be hanged, and thirty of his family with him, who never expected such a death.

CX

The battle is crushing and tremendous. Oliver and Roland fight magnificently, the Archbishop strikes a thousand blows and more, the twelve peers never pause for breath, and the French fight as one man. The pagans die by hundreds and thousands and their only safety is in flight. Their days are cut off, whether it meets their pleasure or not.

The French lose the very pillars of their strength, knights who will never again see their fathers or their families, or Charlemagne, who is waiting for them in the pass.

And in France a terrible uproar breaks loose: a storm of thunder and wind, with rain and hail falling in cloudbursts. There is scarcely a pause between the strokes of lightning, and indeed the earth quakes. From Saint Michael of Peril to Sens, from Besançon to the port of Guitsand, there is not a house without a broken wall. At high noon there is a great darkness and no light at all except when the sky is split with lightning, and no man sees it without terrible dread. Some say:

"This is the last day, and the end of the world has come."

But they know nothing; there is no truth in their words. For it is the great lamentation of the elements for the death of Roland.

CXI

The French have fought courageously and with a will, and the pagans have been slaughtered by thousands and by multitudes: out of the hundred thousand there are not even two still left alive.

The Archbishop says: "Our men are brave; there are no better under heaven. Our Emperor's noble virtues are written into the Chronicle of the Franks."

They ride over the field, they look for those whom they know, they weep over their kinfolk with sorrow and pity, and with full hearts, and with love.

King Marsiliun with his great host moves out against them.

CXII

Marsiliun advances along a valley with the enormous host which he has assembled. The king has divided his army into twenty battle formations. Their helmets shine, studded with jewels set in gold, and their shields gleam, and their gilt-varnished coats of mail. Seven thousand trumpets sound the charge and the whole countryside echoes with the huge sound.

Then Roland says: "Oliver, my companion, my brother, the traitor Ganelon has sworn that we shall be killed, and his betrayal can no longer be hidden. The Emperor will take a terrible vengeance upon him. But for our part, we have before us a battle so rough and furious that no man ever faced one like it. I will attack them with my sword Durendal, and you, my companion, fall upon them with your blade Halteclere—through how many lands we have borne them, and how many battles we have won with their help! They do not deserve to have a bad song sung of them."

CXIII

Marsiliun, seeing the massacre of his knights, commands the trumpets and horns to sound, and rides forward with the great host of his vassals. In front rides a Saracen named Abisme: there is not a man in that company who is more wicked. He is distinguished for his evils and terrible crimes. He does not believe in God, the son of Saint Mary. He is as black as melted pitch. He prefers treason and murder to all the gold of Galicia. No man ever saw him play or laugh. He is brave, and bold in the extreme, which endears him to the wicked King Marsiliun. He bears a dragon as his device, and his followers rally around it. The

Archbishop hates him on sight, longs to attack him, and says to himself, under his breath:

"That Saracen looks a heretic from head to foot. The best thing would be for me to kill him. I never loved cowards nor cowardice."

CXIV

Mounted on the horse which he took from King Grossaille whom he killed in Denmark, the Archbishop begins the battle. His war horse is swift and spirited, with cupped hooves and flat legs, short in the thigh, broad in the rump, deep-chested and high-backed, with a white tail, a yellow forelock, small ears, and his head fawn-colored all over; when the reins are loosened there is no horse who is his equal. The Archbishop touches him with the spurs, and oh God how bravely he rides forward! Nothing can turn him aside: he charges against Abisme and strikes him on the shield studded with amethysts, topazes, tourmalines and blazing rubies, which a devil in Val Metas had given to the Emir Galafres, who in turn had presented it to Abisme. Turpin strikes him; he does not spare him; and after one blow I do not think the shield was worth a farthing. He chops through the body from one side to the other and knocks the corpse onto the bare ground.

The French say: "That was a noble stroke! The cross will not suffer while the Archbishop is there to protect it."

CXV

Now the French can see the full size of the pagan host, spreading over the entire plain. Again and again they call upon Oliver and Roland and the twelve peers to lead them to a place of safety. And the Archbishop speaks his mind to them:

"My lords, barons, do not give way to ignoble thoughts! In the name of God I beg you, do not flee; do not prompt them to sing contemptuously of our courage. It is far better that we should die fighting, for we are told that our end will be soon in any case, and we shall not survive that day, but of one thing I can assure you: the sacred land of Paradise stands open to receive you and you will be seated beside the Holy Innocents."

At these words the French rejoice, and as one man they raise the shout of "Mountjoy!"

CXVI

There was a Saracen there who was lord of half the city of Saragossa; his name was Climborin, a vile and ignoble man. It was he who received the oath of Count Ganelon and afterwards kissed him on the mouth and gave him his helmet and his ruby. He has boasted that he will bring shame upon the "Land of the Fathers" and that he will relieve the Emperor of his crown. He is mounted on his horse Barbamusche, which is swifter than any sparrow hawk or swallow; he digs in his spurs, slackens the reins, and charges against Engeler of Gascony, whose shield and coat of mail are powerless to protect him. The pagan stabs him with his spear, runs him through so that the blade emerges through the other side of his body, and tips his corpse into the field a spear's length away. Then he shouts:

"This rabble is ours to destroy! Charge, pagans, and break their ranks!"

The French say: "Oh God, what a brave knight we have lost!"

CXVII

Count Roland calls to Oliver: "My lord, companion, now Engeler is dead, and we had no braver knight."

Oliver answers: "God grant that I may avenge him!"

He strikes his horse with his spurs of pure gold, grips Halteclere, its blade running with blood, and with immense force strikes the pagan. He wrenches the sword loose and the Saracen falls, and the Adversary carries away his soul. After that he kills Duke Alphaien, splits Escababi's head, and unhorses seven Arabs—they will never be of use again in a battle.

Roland says: "My companion is angry! He is worthy of his fame which is coupled with my own. It is for fighting like that that Charles loves us."

Then he shouts aloud: "Strike them, knights!"

CXVIII

On another side there is a pagan named Valdabrun, King Marsiliun's godfather. He is the lord, at sea, of four hundred galleys, and every sailor on those vessels is a bondsman of his. He had taken Jerusalem by treachery and violated the temple of Solomon, murdering the patriarch beside the font. He is the one who, having received Count Ganelon's promise, gave him his own sword and a thousand gold pieces. Mounted on his horse named Gramimund, which is more swift and nimble than any falcon, he digs in his sharp spurs and charges forward to attack the rich Duke Sansun, breaks his shield, rends his hauberk, drives the tails of his pennon into the Duke's body, and flings him, dead, a good spear's length away from his saddle.

"Strike them, pagans, for we are sure of victory!"

The French say: "Oh God, we have lost a brave knight!"

CXIX

You may know that when Count Roland sees that Sansun is dead he is filled with grief, and with Durendal in his hand, which is worth more than its weight in fine gold, he spurs his horse and charges furiously at the pagan. With all his might the brave Count bears down upon the other and his blow falls on the helmet studded with jewels set in gold, splits the head and the coat of mail and the body and the good saddle studded with jewels set in gold, and cleaves deep into the horse's back. He kills both horse and rider, for what blame or praise it may be worth.

The pagans say: "That stroke was a bitter one for us!"

Roland answers: "I have no fondness for you, vainglorious as you are, and in the wrong."

CXX

There is an African there, come from Africa, whose name is Malquiant, King Malcud's son. His armor is planted all over with gold and shines to heaven above all the rest. Mounted on his horse called Saut-Perdu, who has no peer for speed, he charges against Anseis and strikes him on the shield. He cuts through the crimson and azure blazon, breaks the skirts of his hauberk and jams into the body both the head and the shaft of his spear. The Count is dead. His days are ended.

The French say: "Noble knight, we grieve for you."

CXXI

Turpin the Archbishop rides over the field—no tonsured priest who ever sang mass could put his body to so brave and warlike a use.

He says to the pagan: "God load you with every misfortune! You have killed a man whom my heart mourns for."

He urges forward his good horse, strikes the pagan on his Toledo shield, and hurls the corpse onto the green grass.

CXXII

On another side there is a pagan named Grandonies, who is the son of Capuel, the King of Cappadocia. Mounted on a horse called Marmorle, which is more swift and nimble than any bird that flies, he slackens the reins, digs in his spurs, and rides out to strike Gerin with great force, breaking his vermilion shield and tearing it from his neck, shearing away his coat of chain mail, and driving his blue pennon into the body, then hurling the corpse onto a high rock. After that the pagan kills Gerin's companion Gerer, and Berenger, and Guiun of Saint Anthony, and then turns to attack a rich duke named Austorie, lord of Valence and Envers-on-Rhone, and hurls him to the ground, dead, to the great rejoicing of the pagans.

The French say: "What a loss to our company!"

CXXIII

Count Roland grips his blood-drenched sword. He has heard the dismayed exclamations of the French, and his own heart is bursting with grief.

He says to the pagan: "God visit all misfortunes upon you! You have killed a man for whose death I will make you pay dearly!"

He spurs his horse and it leaps forward. One knight or the other must triumph, for now they have come together.

CXXIV

Gradonies was bold and brave, a strong and intrepid fighter. Now he finds himself faced with Roland. And though he has never seen him before, he recognizes him by his proud face, his noble body, his regard, his bearing, and he is filled with an uncontrollable dread and tries to escape, but fails, for the Count strikes him with such force that the blow splits his helmet, nose piece and all, cleaves through his nose, and his mouth, and his teeth, and his whole body and the coat of linked chain mail encasing it, the gilded saddle, both sides of the silver saddle tree, and deep into the horse's back. He kills them both; nothing could have saved them. And the knights from Spain all cry out in their grief.

The French say: "He strikes hard, our champion!"

CXXV

The battle is awesome and furious; the French strike with zeal and rage, cutting through wrists, bodies, spines, piercing garments to carve into living flesh. And the bright blood flows onto the green grass.

" 'Land Of The Fathers,' Mahomet's curse upon you! There is no people on earth which can match yours for bravery!"

And there is not a pagan there who does not cry out: "Marsiliun! Ride forward, King! We are in need of help!"

CXXVI

The battle is awesome and vast; the French fight hard with their burnished spears. There you would have seen terrible suffering, so many men maimed and bleeding, lying piled on each other, face up, face down. The Saracens can endure it no longer, and whatever their resolutions may have been, they forsake the field. The French, with all their strength, pursue them.

CXXVII

Count Roland calls out to Oliver: "My lord, companion, surely you must admit that the Archbishop makes a magnificent knight— there is none better on earth under heaven. He knows how to put both his spear and his lance to good use."

"And for that very reason," Count Oliver answers, "let us lend him our help!"

At his words the Franks renew their efforts, and the blows are deadly, the struggle is fierce and bloody, and the Christians suffer heavily. There you would have seen Roland and Oliver cleaving and hacking with their swords, and the Archbishop lunging with his spear. The number of those whom they killed can be determined, for it is written in the records and the accounts, and the Chronicle says that there were more than four thousand. Through the first four assaults they hold their ground and acquit themselves well, but the fifth presses them hard and taxes them severely: all of the French knights are killed except sixty, whom God still spares. Before they die the pagans will have had to pay dearly for their lives.

CXXVIII

When Count Roland sees the slaughter of his knights he calls to his companion, Oliver:

"Fair sir, dear companion, in God's name what do you think now, seeing so many good vassals lying on the ground? We may well mourn for sweet fair France, which is despoiled of such noble knights as these! Oh King, my friend, I grieve that you are not here. Oliver, my brother, what can we do? How can we send word?"

Oliver says: "I do not know. I would rather die than bring shame upon us."

CXXIX

Then Roland says: "I will sound my ivory horn and Charles will hear it as he makes his way through the pass, and the Franks, I promise you, will return."

Oliver says: "That would bring great shame and opprobrium on all your kin, which they would have to bear for the rest of their lives. When I asked you to do it you refused. If you do it now it will not be at my bidding. There would be no bravery in sounding your horn. But look: both your arms are running with blood!"

Count Roland answers: "I have dealt heavy blows."

CXXX

Then Roland says: "The battle is fierce. I will sound my horn and King Charles will hear it."

Oliver says: "That would be an ignoble action! When I asked you to sound a blast, companion, you would not deign to do it. If the King had been here no harm would have come to us. Those knights lying there on the ground cannot be blamed."

Oliver says: "I swear by my beard that if ever again I see lovely Alde, my sister, you may give up all hope of lying in her arms!"

CXXXI

Then Roland says: "Why are you angry with me?"

And he answers: "Companion, it is your own doing, for knightly courage used with prudence is one thing and folly is another, and tempered judgment is more to be valued than the rashness of arrogance. Those French are dead because of your heedlessness, and we will never act again in Charles' service. If you had listened to me my lord would have returned and we would have won this battle and King Marsiliun would have been captured or killed. Woe to us, Roland, that we ever saw your bravery! Charles the Great, a man whose like will never be seen again until God judges the world, will no longer be able to rely on our help, and you will die, and shame will come to France. Today our faithful friendship will end, and before evening we will have parted in sorrow."

CXXXII

The Archbishop has heard their argument, and he sets his spurs of fine gold to his horse and rides over to them and reproaches them:

"My lord Roland, and you, my lord Oliver, in the name of God I beg you, do not fall to quarreling! It is too late for a blast of the horn to save us, but it would be best if you were to blow it nevertheless, for the King will then return and avenge our deaths, and those who have come from Spain must not be allowed to leave the field rejoicing. Our French will dismount, they will find us dead and our bodies mangled, and they will lift us onto biers on the backs of pack mules, and will weep for us in sorrow and pity, and bury us in the aisles of minsters, and we will not be eaten by wolves or pigs or dogs."

Roland answers: "My lord, what you say is wise."

CXXXIII

Roland has set his ivory horn to his mouth; he puts his lips hard against it and blows with all his strength. The mountains are high, and over them the voice of the horn rings long, and more than thirty leagues away its echo answers. Charles hears it, and all the knights in his company.

The King says: "Our men are fighting!"

And Ganelon, contradicting him, answers: "If anyone else had said so I would say he was lying."

CXXXIV

Count Roland, in pain and anguish, and in great sorrow, blows a blast on his ivory horn, and the bright blood flows from his mouth, and the veins burst on his forehead, but the sound of the horn swells and mounts, and Charles hears it as he makes his way through the pass, and Duke Naimes hears it, and it comes to the ears of the Franks.

Then the King says: "I hear the sound of Roland's horn, and he would not blow it unless there were a battle."

Ganelon answers: "Battle? There is no battle! You are old and your beard and hair are white and flowery, and when you speak like that you sound like a child. You are well aware of Roland's vast pride—it is a wonder that God has endured him for so long. Did he not seize Noples without waiting for your command? The Saracens rode out on that occasion and joined battle with Roland, and that good vassal flooded the meadows afterwards to wash away the gory remains ... A single rabbit has been known to set him blowing his horn from one end of the day to the other. At the moment he is performing some kind of sport before his peers. Who under heaven would dare to take the field against him? Ride on! Why should you pause? The 'Land of the Fathers' is still a long way off."

CXXXV

Count Roland's mouth is streaming blood and the veins on his forehead have burst. In sorrow and pain he blows his ivory horn. Charles hears it, and his French hear it.

Then the King says: "That horn has a long breath!"

Duke Naimes answers: "Some knight is in anguish. There is a battle, I am sure of it, and he who has betrayed the knights in the rear guard is the same who now counsels you to fail them. Arm, sound your battle cry, and go to the help of your noble followers. You have heard enough. That horn is the sound of Roland's despair!"

CXXXVI

The Emperor has commanded them to sound their horns, and the French dismount and put on their coats of mail and their helmets, and gird on their swords chased with gold. They have resplendent shields and large strong spears with white and vermilion and blue pennons. All the knights in that host mount their war horses and spur them along the pass, saying to each other:

"If we can get to Roland before he dies, together we will deal them great blows!"

What good are their words? For they have waited too long.

CXXXVII

The evening lengthens, the day draws out, and their armor shines against the sun, their hauberks and helmets flashing fire, and their shields also, which are elaborately painted with flowers, and their spears with the pennons worked in gold. The Emperor rides on in wrath, and the French in sorrow and rage, and there is not one of them who is not weeping bitterly, in fear for Roland. The King has bidden them seize Ganelon, and turns him over to the cooks of the royal household, whose chief, a man named Besgun, he summons to his presence:

"Guard him well for me, as a villain like that ought to be guarded. He has betrayed vassals of my own household."

They take the traitor and surround him with a hundred kitchen hands of the best and the worst, and tear out his beard and mustache, and each one of them gives him four blows of his fist; they beat him soundly with clubs and staves, and put a chain on his neck as though he were a bear, and they fling him over a pack mule to shame him. They guard him in this way until the day when they give him back to Charles.

CXXXVIII

The peaks are high and dark and huge, the valleys deep, and the torrents dash through them. They sound their trumpets at the head of the column and at the rear, and all together blare in answer to Roland's ivory horn. The Emperor rides on, wrathfully, and the French ride on in rage and sorrow, and there is not one of them who is not weeping grievously and praying to God to protect Roland until they reach the battlefield; then indeed he and they will strike together. But what good is their talk? Their words are useless. They have waited too long. They will be too late.

CXXXIX

Charles the King rides on in great wrath, with his white beard spread out over his chain mail, and all the knights of France spurring forward around him. There is not one of them who does not furiously lament that he is not with Roland the captain, who is fighting against the Saracens of Spain, and who is in such agony that his soul cannot remain much longer in his body. Oh God, what fighters they are, those sixty knights in his company! No better men ever served king or captain.

CXL

Roland gazes at the mountains and the hillsides, and there he sees so many French dead lying, and as a noble knight he weeps for them:
"My lords, barons, God have mercy upon you and admit your souls without exception into Paradise and lay you down on the holy flowers. I never saw better vassals than you were, who have served me for so long without respite and have conquered so vast a domain in the name of Charles! The Emperor brought you up to sorrow. And you, land of France who have no peer for sweetness, today you are made desolate by calamity! Barons of France, I see you dying for my sake and I cannot defend you nor protect you. May God, who never lied, be your

help! Brother Oliver, I must not fail you. I will die of sorrow if nothing else kills me. My lord, companion, let us strike them again!"

CXLI

Count Roland has returned to the battle, and with Durendal in his fist he strikes blows worthy of a knight. He has hewn in half Faldrun of Pui and twenty-four others from among the pick of the Saracens. No man ever burned so to avenge himself. As stags before the dogs the pagans run before Roland. The Archbishop says:

"You have fought well! That is the kind of courage which a knight should have who bears arms and bestrides a good horse. He must be strong and overbearing in battle or he is not worth a farthing and would do better as a monk in some monastery praying daily for our sins."

Roland answers: "Strike, and do not spare them!"

At this word the Franks resume the battle. The Christians suffer terrible losses.

CXLII

In a battle such as this one where it is known that no prisoners will be taken, the knights defend themselves furiously, and for this reason the Franks are as fierce as lions. And now Marsiliun himself approaches as a knight. He is mounted on his horse named Gaignun. He digs in his spurs and rides to strike Bevun, the lord of Belne and Digun. He breaks his shield, smashes through his hauberk, and hurls him down, dead, without another stroke. Then he kills Yvoerie and Ivun, and Gerard of Roussillon with them. Count Roland is not far away, and he says to the pagan:

"May the Lord God lay his curse upon you, who have villainously slaughtered so many of my companions! Before we part you will have been dealt a blow and will have learned the name of my sword!"

Like a true knight the Count rides to strike him and slices off his right hand. Then he turns to Jurfaleu the Blond, the son of King Marsiliun, and cuts off his head. The pagans shout:

"Help us, Mahomet! And you, our gods, for our sake wreak vengeance upon Charles, who has stocked this land with evil men who would rather die than quit the field!"

One of them says to the other: "Let us flee!" And at that word a hundred thousand take to flight, and will not return, whoever calls.

CXLIII

And what difference will it make? For even if Marsiliun himself flees there is still his uncle Marganice, the lord of Carthage, Alfrere, Garmalia and Ethiopia, an accursèd country. The black races are under his command. They have large noses and broad ears. There are more than fifty thousand of them. They ride fiercely, furiously, and they shout the pagan battle cry. Then Roland says:

"Here is our death bearing down upon us, and now I know beyond any doubt that we can live no longer. But he is a traitor who does not sell his life dearly! Strike, my lords, with your polished blades, and contend for your lives and your deaths, so that sweet France may not be shamed on our account! When Charles my lord comes to this field he will see that such punishment has been wrought on the Saracens that for every one of our dead there are fifteen of theirs, and he will not fail to pronounce his blessing over us."

CXLIV

When Roland sees the accursed people who are blacker than ink, with nothing white about them except their teeth, the Count says:

"Now I know beyond any doubt that we shall die today. Now I am sure. Strike, French knights, for now I lead you once more against them!"

Oliver says: "A curse upon the slowest!"

At this word the French charge into them.

CXLV

When the pagans see how few of the French are left they feel proud; they take heart. They say to each other:

"The Emperor is in the wrong."

Marganice, mounted on a sorrel horse, digs in his golden spurs and strikes Oliver from behind, in the middle of his back. The shining hauberk parts, laying bare the body, and the spear passes through and out at the breast. Then the pagan says:

"You were hit hard that time! Charles the Great left you here in the pass to your sorrow! He has done us wrong, but he will have no reason to congratulate himself, for in your death alone I have avenged all of ours."

CXLVI

Oliver knows that he has been given a deadly wound, and he grips Halteclere and with its burnished blade strikes Marganice on the sharp-pointed golden helmet, smashes through its flowers and gems and cleaves the head from here down to the front teeth. He gives the sword a wrench and hurls down the corpse. And then he says:

"A curse on you, pagan! I cannot say that Charles has suffered no loss, but you at least will never go back to the kingdom from which you came and brag to any wife or woman that you left me the poorer by so much as a farthing, nor that you did me or anyone else any harm!"

Then he calls to Roland to come to his help.

CXLVII

Oliver knows that he has been dealt a mortal wound and his passion to avenge himself is insatiable. He charges into the thick of the pagans, striking out like a brave knight, shearing through the shafts of their spears, and their shields and their feet and their wrists and their saddles and their ribs. Any man who had seen him then dismembering Saracens, flinging corpse upon corpse, would have been able to remember a noble knight. He does not neglect to raise Charles' battle cry, but shouts, "Mountjoy!" loud and clear. He calls to his friend and his peer, Roland:

"My lord, companion, come to my side, for today in bitter grief we must separate."

CXLVIII

Roland looks at Oliver's face and sees that it has turned gray, livid, colorless, and pale, and he sees the bright blood streaking down Oliver's body and falling in streams to the ground. The Count says:

"Oh God, what can I do now! My lord, my companion, your courage has been brought to grief, and no man will ever be your equal. Ah sweet France, what a loss of noble knights you have suffered today, and how stricken and wasted you are now! What a heavy blow this will be to the Emperor!"

And with these words he faints on his horse.

CXLIX

Look now: Roland has fainted on his horse and Oliver has been dealt a mortal wound and has lost so much blood that his sight has become confused. He can no longer see anything clearly, whether it is far away or near. He can no longer recognize any living man, and finding his companion in front of him, he strikes with all his strength at the helmet with its jewels set in gold, and he splits it down to the nose piece but does not touch the head. Roland, when the blow has struck him, looks Oliver in the face and softly and gently asks him:

"My lord, companion, did you mean to strike me? It is I, Roland, who have loved you dearly for so long. You never warned me nor challenged me."

Oliver says: "Now I hear you speak, but I cannot see you. May the Lord God keep you in His sight! I have struck you and I beg you to forgive me!"

Roland answers: "I have suffered no harm. Here and before God I forgive you."

With these words they bow to each other.

And look: it is thus, tenderly, that they part.

CL

Oliver feels the pains of death encroaching upon him. His eyes reel in his head. He loses his hearing. He can no longer see anything. He dismounts and reclines on the ground, and there in a loud voice, with his hands clasped and lifted up toward heaven, he confesses his sins and prays to God to receive him into Paradise, and he blesses Charles and sweet France and above all other men his companion Roland. His heart fails, his helmet sags, his whole body slumps onto the earth. The Count is dead. He is there no longer. Roland, that brave knight, weeps for him and gives way to his grief. Never in this world will you hear a more sorrowful man.

CLI

Now Roland sees that his friend is dead and lying face down on the ground, and with great tenderness he speaks his lament and farewell:

"My lord, companion, your tempered courage has been brought to grief! We have been together for days and years and you never did me any wrong, and I never did you any, and now that you are dead it is a grief to me to be alive."

At this word Roland, the baron, faints, sitting on Veillantif his horse, and his stirrups of fine gold hold him up, so that whichever way he leans he cannot fall.

CLII

Before Roland returns to himself and recovers from his faint, terrible losses have been inflicted on his force, for the French are dead, they are all lost except the Archbishop and Gualter of Hum. Gualter has come down from the heights. He has fought hard against the Saracens of Spain; all his men are dead, overwhelmed by the pagans, and whether he wishes to or not he flees toward the valleys there and calls out to Roland to help him:

"Ah noble Count, man of courage, where are you? I was never afraid where you were. It is I, Gualter, who conquered Maelgut! It is I, the nephew of old white-haired Droun, and you used to love me for my courage. My lance is splintered, my shield is pierced, my hauberk is broken and rent, and as for my body . . . I will die in any case, but I have sold my life dearly."

Roland hears these words, and he spurs his horse and rides toward Gualter.

CLIII

Roland, in his grief and his rage, strikes into the midst of the pagans and hurls down twenty of the Saracens of Spain, dead. And Gualter kills six, and the Archbishop five. The pagans say:

"These men are monstrous! Lords, take care that they do not get away alive! Any man who does not attack them now is a traitor, and he who lets them escape is a coward!"

Then they renew the hue and cry and ride to attack from all sides.

CLIV

Count Roland is a noble warrior, Gualter of Hum is a superb knight, and the Archbishop is a brave and proven fighter. None of them would forsake the others on any account, and they charge into the midst of the pagans. A thousand Saracens dismount, and there are forty thousand on horses, and I swear it, they are afraid to approach. Instead they throw lances and spears, and bolts and javelins and arrows and sharp missiles and long darts. One of the first of these kills Gualter. Turpin of Reims has his shield pierced by another. And then another smashes his helmet and passes through to wound him in the head, and his hauberk is rent and broken, and four spears pass through his body. They kill his war horse under him. Now there is cause for grief, as the Archbishop falls.

CLV

Turpin of Reims knows that he has been mortally wounded. Four spears have passed through his body. That brave peer gets to his feet again, looks for Roland, runs to him, and says:

"I am not beaten! A good vassal never yields while there is still life in him."

He draws his sword Almace, with its burnished blade, and in the thick of the pagans he strikes a thousand blows and more. Charles said afterwards that Turpin of Reims spared none of the pagans, for he found four hundred of them lying around the Archbishop, some wounded, some cleft in two, some headless. That is what the Chronicle says, which was written by one who had seen the field: the worthy Gilie, for whom God performed wonders. He wrote the account in the monastery of Laon, and any man who does not know that is ignorant of the whole story.

CLVI

Count Roland fights nobly, but his body is hot and running with sweat, and his head has been throbbing with fierce pains since he blew his horn and the veins burst on his temples. But he wants to know whether Charles is on his way, and he takes his ivory horn and blows it, feebly. The Emperor halts and listens.

"My lords," he says, "it is going badly for us! Today Roland, my nephew, is lost to us. From the sound of his horn I can tell that he does not have much longer to live. Any man who hopes to find him alive must ride fast. Now sound every trumpet in this host!"

Sixty thousand trumpets blare, and the sound crashes through the mountains, and the valleys echo. The pagans hear that note, and they are not moved to laughter. They say to each other:

"Charles is upon us!"

CLVII

The pagans say: "The Emperor is returning! Listen: you can hear the trumpets of the French! If Charles comes our losses will be heavy, and Roland, if he survives, will renew the war, and our land of Spain will be lost to us."

Four hundred of them who pride themselves on being the best fighters in the field, mass together, helmet by helmet, to launch a single fierce, crushing attack on Roland.

This time the Count will have no leisure.

CLVIII

Count Roland sees them coming and his strength and pride and courage mount. He will never yield to them as long as there is life in him. Astride his horse whom men call Veillantif, he digs in his spurs of fine gold and charges into the thick of them, and Turpin, the Archbishop, with him.

The pagans say to each other: "Now let us go, friend! We have heard the horns of the knights of France, and Charles, the mighty King, is returning."

CLIX

Count Roland never loved a coward, nor a proud man, nor a man of ill will, nor any knight who was not a brave fighter. He calls to Archbishop Turpin:

"My lord, you are on foot and I am mounted, and out of love for you I will stay beside you and together we will take what comes, good or evil, and no man made of flesh will force me from you. Let us go together to attack the pagans. Durendal still strikes hardest!"

The Archbishop says: "He who holds back now is a traitor! Charles is returning. He will avenge us."

CLX

The pagans say: "Woe to us that we were ever born! What an evil day has now risen above us! We have lost our lords and our peers. Charles the brave is returning with his great host and we can hear the clear trumpets of the knights of France, and the shout of 'Mountjoy' rings loud in our ears. Such is the fierce bravery of Count Roland that no man made of flesh will overcome him. Let us hurl our weapons at him and then leave him where he is."

And they throw javelins at him in great numbers, and spears and lances and feathered darts, and they have pierced Roland's shield and smashed it, and broken and rent his hauberk, but their weapons have not touched his body. But Veillantif is wounded in thirty places: they have killed the Count's horse under him. The pagans flee, leaving him on the field. Count Roland is left there, on foot.

CLXI

Smarting with anger and rage, the pagans flee headlong toward Spain, and Count Roland, having lost Veillantif and been forced to dismount whether he likes it or not, cannot give chase. He goes to Archbishop Turpin to help him, unlaces the gold helmet from his head, draws the light, shining hauberk from his body, and cuts his tunic to pieces, which he stuffs into the gaping wounds. Then he draws the Archbishop to his breast and gently lays him down on the green grass. Then tenderly Roland begs a favor of him:

"Ah noble lord, give me leave to go from you! Our companions who were so dear to us are dead now, and we should not leave them where they are. Let me go and look for them and identify them, and bring them here before you and arrange them in a row."

The Archbishop says: "Go and return! The field is yours—I thank God—yours and mine."

CLXII

Roland leaves him and goes off over the field alone, through the valleys, along the mountains, looking ... There he finds Yvoerie and Ivun, and after him Engeler of Gascony. There he finds Gerin, and Gerer his companion, and Berenger and Otun. There he finds Anseis and Sansun, and after them Gerard the Old, from Roussillon. One by one he takes them up, that brave knight, and brings them all to the Archbishop, and sets them in a row before his knees, and the Archbishop cannot hold back the tears. He lifts up his hand and offers a benediction, and then he says:

"My lords, you were brought to grief, and now may God the Glorious receive your souls every one and lay them on the holy flowers in Paradise! Now the pains of my own death are upon me and I will never again see the Emperor in his might."

CLXIII

Roland leaves him and goes off over the field, looking. And he has found his companion, Oliver. He draws him to his breast, in his arms, and makes his way to the Archbishop as best he can, and lays Oliver on a shield beside the others, and the Archbishop absolves him and blesses him. Then sorrow and pity well up, and then Roland says:

"Fair companion, Oliver, you were the son of Duke Reiner who ruled the marches of the Valley of Runers. To shatter a lance and pierce a shield, to strike down the proud and fill them with terror, and to sustain the brave and give them counsel, and to strike down base and vile men and fill them with terror, there is no better knight in any country."

CLXIV

When Count Roland sees all the peers dead, and Oliver whom he had loved so dearly, tenderness wells up in him and he begins to weep. His face has grown pale, and his sorrow is so great that he cannot keep to his feet any longer, but his will forsakes him and he falls to the ground in a faint. The Archbishop says:

"Brave knight, I grieve for you!"

CLXV

When the Archbishop sees Roland fall down in a faint his sorrow becomes even greater than it had been at any time before. He stretches out his hand and takes the ivory horn.

There is a stream at Roncesvalles, and the Archbishop wants to fetch some water to Roland. He walks away with little steps, swaying on his feet, so weak that he cannot go forward, having lost so much blood that all the strength has gone out of him, and after less time than it takes a man to cross an acre of ground his heart fails him, he falls forward, and the terrible agony of his death seizes him.

CLXVI

Count Roland recovers from his faint and gets to his feet, though in great pain, and looks around him, down along the valleys, up to the mountains, over the green grass, beyond his companions. And he sees on the ground that noble knight, the Archbishop, who had been ordained in the name of God. Gazing upwards, with his clasped hands lifted toward heaven, the Archbishop makes his confession and prays to God to receive him into Paradise. Now Turpin, Charles' warrior, is dead. In great battles and in beautiful sermons, all his life he was a champion of Christendom against the pagans. May God grant him His holy blessing!

CLXVII

Count Roland sees the Archbishop on the ground and the bowels sagging out of his body and the brain oozing over his forehead. On the breast, between the two collarbones, he crosses the white and shapely hands. Then, following the custom of his country, Roland speaks a lament over him:

"Ah noble sir, knight born of honored ancestors, today I commend you to the Glorious King of Heaven. No man ever served him with a better will. Never since the days of the saints was there such a man of God for maintaining the laws and drawing men to the faith. May your soul not suffer, and may the door of Paradise be open to you!"

CLXVIII

Now Roland feels death near him. His brains have begun to seep out through his ears. He prays for the peers, asking God to summon them to His presence, and then for himself he calls upon the angel Gabriel. He takes his ivory horn, so that no one may be able to bring shame on him by showing it, and in the other hand he takes his sword Durendal. A little farther away than a man might shoot with a crossbow, on the side toward Spain, there is a grassy place. Roland goes to it and climbs a little mound. There is a beautiful tree there and there are four great stones of marble under it. On the green grass he has fallen backward, and he has fainted there, for death is near him.

CLXIX

The mountains are high, and the trees are tall, and there are four great stones of marble there, shining. Count Roland faints on the green grass.

A Saracen has been watching him closely from among the corpses, where he has been lying with his body and face smeared with blood, pretending to be dead. He gets to his feet and begins to run. He is a man of handsome appearance and great courage. It is pride which spurs him on to this fatal folly. He seizes Roland by his arms and body and he says:

"Charles' nephew is beaten! I will take this sword to Arabia."

As he draws it the Count returns somewhat to his senses.

CLXX

Roland feels the sword being taken away from him and he opens his eyes and says to the other:

"You do not look like one of ours."

He grips his ivory horn, which he had not wanted to leave behind, and with it he strikes the pagan on the helmet, which is covered with jewels set in gold, and smashes the steel and the head and the bone so that both the eyes burst from the face and the body falls dead at his feet. Then he says:

"Base pagan, what made you so rash as to seize me, whether by fair means or foul? Whoever hears the story will take you for a fool. But the mouth of my ivory horn is shattered, and the crystal has fallen from it, and the gold."

CLXXI

Now Roland feels the sight of his eyes forsaking him, and with a great effort he gets to his feet. All the color has left his face. He sees before him a gray stone. In sorrow and bitterness he strikes it ten blows with his sword, and the steel grates but will not break nor be blunted.

"Ah," says the Count, "Saint Mary help me! Ah Durendal, my good sword, you have fallen on sad days, for I am dying and you will no longer be in my keeping. With you I have won so many battles in the field and conquered so many broad lands which white-bearded Charles rules over! May you never fall into the hands of any man who will flee before another, for you have been owned by a brave knight for a long time, and holy France will never see another like you."

CLXXII

Next Roland strikes the great blood-red stone, and the steel grates but will not break nor be blunted. When he sees that he cannot break the sword, Roland begins to grieve over it:

"Ah Durendal, how beautiful you are, and how bright, and how dazzling, glittering and flashing in the sunlight! Charles was in the Valley of Moriane when God in heaven sent an angel to tell him to give you to a count, one of his captains, and it was then that you were girded upon me by that noble king, that great king.

"With this I conquered Anjou and Brittany for him, and for him I conquered Poitou and Maine. With this I conquered proud Normandy for him, and for him conquered Provence and Aquitaine and Lombardy and the whole of Romagna. With this I conquered Bavaria and all of Flanders for him, and Burgundy, and Poland from one end to the other, and Constantinople, from which he received homage, and in Saxony his command is obeyed. With this I conquered Scotland for him, and ... and England, which he held as his own place. With this I have conquered so many lands for him, so many countries, and whitebearded Charles rules over them. And now I am full of grief and sorrow because of this sword, for I would rather die than let it fall into the hands of the pagans. God, Father, do not allow France to be thus dishonored!"

CLXXIII

Roland, striking harder than I can say, brings the sword down on a gray stone, and it grates, but is neither chipped nor shattered. It rebounds toward heaven. When the Count sees that it will not be broken, very softly he grieves over it:

"Ah Durendal, how beautiful you are, and how blessed, with the holy relics in your golden hilt—there is a tooth of Saint Peter's there, and some of Saint Basil's blood, and several hairs of my lord Saint Denis, and a bit of a garment of Saint Mary's. It would not be right if you were to fall into the hands of pagans; you should be in the keeping of Christians. May no coward ever possess you! With you I have conquered many broad lands which Charles rules over. His beard is in flower. Because of you the emperor is venerable and mighty."

CLXXIV

Now Roland feels death taking everything from him, descending from his head into his heart, and he runs under a pine tree and lies down with his face to the green grass. Underneath him he places his sword and ivory horn. He turns his head toward the pagans, so that Charles and all his knights may say:

"The noble knight died a conqueror."

He makes his confession, carefully, over and over, and he offers his glove, as a token of his sins, to God.

CLXXV

Now Roland feels that the end of his life has come. He has lain down on a steep hill with his face toward Spain and with one hand he beats his breast:

"God, I acknowledge my guilt and I beg for Thy mercy for all the sins, greater and lesser, which I have committed from the hour of my birth until this day when I lie here overcome by death!"

He has held out his right glove to God.

Angels descend out of heaven and come to him.

CLXXVI

Count Roland has lain down under a pine tree, turning his face toward Spain. Many things come to his memory—so many countries which he had conquered as a brave knight, and sweet France, the land of his ancestors and of Charlemagne, his lord, who had reared him. He cannot hold back the tears and the sighs.

But he does not wish to forget himself. He confesses his sins and prays to God for mercy:

"True Father, who never lied, who raised Saint Lazarus from the dead, and saved Daniel from the lions, save my soul in spite of all the perils which I have incurred with the sins of my life!"

He offers his right glove to God, and Saint Gabriel takes it from his hand. His head sinks onto his arm. With clasped hands he comes to the end of his life. God has sent His angels, Cherubim and Saint Michael of Peril, and Saint Gabriel with them, and they bear the soul of the Count to Paradise.

CLXXVII

Roland is dead and God has taken his soul into heaven.

The Emperor reaches Roncesvalles. There is not a track nor a path, nor a yard nor even a foot of empty ground without a Frank or a pagan lying on it.

Charles calls out: "Where are you, fair nephew? Where is the Archbishop? And Count Oliver? Where is Gerin? And his companion Gerer? Where is Otun? And Count Berenger? Ivun and Yvoerie, who were so dear to me? What has become of Engeler of Gascony? And Duke Sansun? And the brave Anseis? Where is Gerard the Old, from Roussillon? Where are the twelve peers whom I left here?"

What good is it to call? Not one of them answers.

"Oh God!" the King says, "what reason I have now to lament that I was not here when the battle began!"

In his passion he tears at his beard. His brave knights weep. Twenty thousand of them faint to the ground. Duke Neimun is overcome with grief.

CLXXVIII

There is no knight or baron there who is not shaken with grief and bitter weeping. They are weeping for their sons, for their brothers, for their nephews and their friends and for their lords, and many of them faint to the ground out of sorrow. Now Duke Naimes conducts himself worthily, for he is the first to say to the Emperor:

"Look before you. You can see the dust rising over the main roads two leagues away, there are so many of the pagans. Now ride! Avenge this sorrow of ours!"

"Oh God," Charles says, "they are so far already! Now render me the obedience and honor which you owe me, for they have stolen from me the flower of sweet France."

The King summons Gebuin and Otun, Tedbalt of Reims and Count Milun:

"Guard the field, and the valleys, and the mountains. Leave the dead where they are lying and let no beast nor lion touch them. Let no squire nor foot soldier be touched, nor any man be touched until God permits us to return to this field."

And they answer with sweet and loving reverence:

"Just Emperor, dear lord, we shall do it!"

They keep a thousand of their knights with them.

CLXXIX

The Emperor commands the trumpets to sound, and then that brave king rides forward with his enormous host. The Saracens of Spain have turned their backs; the Franks set out in pursuit, all riding together. When the King sees the dusk descending he dismounts on the green grass of a meadow and lies down on the ground and prays to the Lord God to make the sun stand still and the night wait and the day go on. Then an angel who had spoken to him many times before comes and says to him:

"Ride on, Charles, for the light will not fail you. God knows that you have lost the flower of France. You can wreak vengeance upon the evildoers."

When he hears these words the Emperor mounts.

CLXXX

For Charlemagne's sake God has performed a great miracle, for the sun is standing still where it was. The pagans flee and the French give chase furiously and catch them in Val Tenebrus and drive them on toward Saragossa, having cut off the main roads and lanes by which they might have escaped. All along the way the Franks harry them with fierce blows, and slaughter them. Now the pagans are confronted by the deep, awesome and swiftly flowing waters of the Ebro, and there is neither barge there, nor boat, nor galley. The pagans call upon their god Termagant, and then they leap in, but no divinity protects them. Those who are in full armor are the heaviest, and great numbers of them sink to the bottom, and others are swept off by the current, and they are the lucky ones who drink their fill at once, for in fact all of them drown, and in fearful anguish. The French shout:

"Roland, we grieve for you!"

CLXXXI

When Charles sees that all the pagans are dead, many of them killed, and the greater part of them drowned, and when he sees the vast spoils which his knights have taken, the noble King dismounts and lies down on the ground and gives thanks to God. When he stands up again the sun has set. The Emperor says:

"It is time to make camp. It is too late to return to Roncesvalles. Our horses are tired and listless. Take off their saddles. Take the bits from their mouths. Let them refresh themselves in the meadows here."

The Franks say: "Sire, you have spoken wisely."

CLXXXII

The Emperor has pitched his camp. The French dismount in the empty country and take the saddles from their horses and the golden bits out of their mouths and turn them loose in the meadows where there is cool grass in plenty. There is nothing more that they can do for them. Then whoever is tired goes to sleep on the ground. That night no one mounts guard.

CLXXXIII

The Emperor has made his bed in a meadow. The brave King sets his massive spear at his head, not wishing to lay aside his arms that night. He does not remove his shining gilt-varnished hauberk; his helmet, studded with jewels set in gold, is laced to his head, and his sword Joyeuse is girded to his side. There was never another like it. Its brilliance changes color thirty times a day. We have heard of the lance which wounded Our Lord, on the cross: by the goodness of God the point of it has come into Charles' keeping, and he has caused the point of it to be mounted in the golden pommel of his sword. And it is because of this honor and this grace in it that the sword was given the name Joyeuse. The knights of France are not likely to forget it, for from it came their battle cry of "Mountjoy!" and therefore no people can stand against them.

CLXXXIV

The night is clear and the moon is shining. Charles has lain down, but his sorrow for Roland comes over him, and he grieves bitterly for Oliver and the twelve peers, and for the French knights whom he had left in their blood at Roncesvalles. He weeps, he laments, he cannot help it, and he prays to God to save their souls. The King is tired, he is weighed down with heavy grief, and he sleeps because he can no longer stay awake. And over all those meadows the Franks lie sleeping. Not one horse is able to keep to its feet. Those that want grass crop it lying down.

He who has endured great suffering has learned much.

CLXXXV

Charles sleeps the sleep of the weary. God sends Saint Gabriel to keep watch over the Emperor, and all night the angel stands at his head, and by means of a vision, whose significance is made plain in terrible omens, foretells a battle which will be fought against him.

Charles looks up toward heaven and sees thunderbolts, hail, rushing winds, storms and awesome tempests, and fires and flames appear to him, falling suddenly upon his whole army. The lances of ash wood and of apple wood catch fire and burn, and the shields, even to the gold bosses on them. And the shafts of their sharp spears are splintered, and their hauberks and their steel helmets are broken; and he sees his knights in great distress. Then bears and leopards come to devour them, serpents and vipers, dragons and devils, and more than thirty thousand griffons, and all of them fling themselves on the French. And the French cry out:

"Charlemagne, help us!"

The King is filled with sorrow and pity. He longs to go to their help, but he cannot, for his way is blocked by a huge lion which comes out of a wood toward him, raging and proud and fierce, and springs at his body and seizes him, and they fall to grips and struggle and he cannot say which of them is on top and which of them is underneath. And the Emperor does not wake.

CLXXXVI

After that, another vision comes to him: he is in France, at Aix, on a dais, and is holding a bear by two chains. He sees thirty other bears emerge from the Ardenne and come toward him, each one talking like a man. They say to him:

"Sire, give him back to us! It is not right that you should keep him for so long. He is our own kin, and we are bound to come to his help."

Out of his palace a greyhound dashes, and choosing the largest of the bears, on the green grass, beyond its companions, attacks it. Then the King sees a fearful combat, but he cannot tell which of them wins and which is beaten.

This is what the angel shows to the noble lord. Charles sleeps on until the morning, and the bright day.

CLXXXVII

King Marsiliun flees to Saragossa, and there he dismounts in the shade of an olive tree. His sword is broken, and his helmet, and his coat of mail, and he lies down in wretchedness on the green grass. He has lost the whole of his right hand, and he faints from pain and loss of blood. Bramimunde, his wife, comes before him, weeping and crying out, and uttering loud laments, and there are more than twenty thousand men with her, all of them cursing Charles and sweet France. And they run to the image of Apollin which is in the crypt there, and fall to berating it and horribly abusing it:

"Oh wicked god, why have you visited such shame upon us? Why have you allowed our King to be overthrown? Let a man give you long and faithful service and you will give him an ill reward!"

Then they strip from it its scepter and its crown, and hang it by the hands on a column, and topple it into the dirt among their feet, and beat it and smash it with clubs. And they tear out Termagant's carbuncle and hurl the image of Mahomet into a ditch for pigs and dogs to devour and befoul.

CLXXXVIII

Marsiliun recovers from his faint and has himself carried into his vaulted bedroom, painted and inscribed in many colors. And Bramimunde, the Queen, weeps because of him, and tears her hair, and calls herself a wretch, and cries out, shrieking every word:

"Oh Saragossa, now you are bereft of that noble king who had you in his keeping! Our gods have betrayed us, for this morning they failed him in battle. And the Emir is a coward if he does not come now and fight with these bold people who are so proud that they are careless of their lives. The Emperor with the flowering beard is brave; he is foolhardy. He will never flee from a battle. Oh what a pity that someone does not kill him!"

CLXXXIX

The Emperor, by the exercise of his great power, has stayed seven whole years in Spain and taken castles and many cities, though Marsiliun has made every effort to resist. Ever since the first year the Sara-

cen King has been sending sealed messages to Babylon, to the ancient
Emir Baligant, who has survived both Virgil and Homer, urging him to
come to the relief of Saragossa. Otherwise, the messages continue,
Baligant's gods and all the idols which he adores will be abandoned,
and Marsiliun will accept Christianity and come to terms with
Charlemagne. But Baligant is far away, and he has taken a long time.
He has gathered together his people from out of forty kingdoms, and
he has had his great transport vessels made ready, and has equipped
barges and galleys and ships. Below Alexandria there is a port giving
onto the sea, and there he has assembled his entire fleet. It is in May,
on the first day of summer, that he embarks with his whole army.

CXC

That race of the devil is sending an enormous host.
They scud along with sails and oars, maintaining their course, and
their mastheads and their tall prows gleam with carbuncles and
lanterns which flash so brightly into the sky that at night they adorn
the sea. And as the vessels approach the land of Spain, this brilliance
floods the whole coast, so that it shines.
The news of their arrival reaches Marsiliun.

CXCI

Rather than anchor, the pagans sail on and, leaving the sea, enter
fresh water, sail past Marbrise and Marbrose, and ascend the Ebro with
their entire fleet, which is spangled with lanterns and carbuncles so
that it gleams brightly all night. With daylight they sail on to Saragossa.

CXCII

The day is clear, with brilliant sunlight. The Emir has disembarked
from his vessel. On his right he is escorted by Espaneliz, and seventeen
kings follow behind him, and more counts and dukes than I can say.

Under a laurel tree which is growing in the middle of the camp they toss a white silk robe onto the green grass, and on it they place an ivory throne, and on that Baligant the pagan is seated. All the others remain standing. Their lord speaks first:

"Brave and open-hearted knights, listen now to what I have to say! Charles the King, the Emperor of the Franks, has no right even to eat except at my command, and he has waged a great war against me throughout all of Spain. I will march into sweet France and seek him out, and the war will not end in my lifetime except with his death or his admission of defeat."

He strikes his knee with his right glove.

CXCIII

And having said it, he is as good as his word, and all the gold under heaven would not dissuade him from going to Aix, where Charles is holding court. And his men applaud his decision and advise the same thing. Then he summons two of his knights, one named Clarifan and the other Clarien.

"I command you, the sons of King Maltraien who in the old days was happy to be my ambassador, to go to Saragossa and inform King Marsiliun, in my name, that I have come to help him against the French. If I can come face to face with them there will be a great battle. Give him this folded glove threaded with gold, and tell him to wear it on his right fist. Take him this staff of pure gold and tell him to come and acknowledge his fealty to me. I will go to France and carry the war to Charles, who will either kneel at my feet and beg for mercy, and renounce the Christian faith, or else I will take the crown from his head."

"Sire," the pagans answer, "you have spoken well."

CXCIV

Baligant says: "My lords, to your horses! Let one take the glove and the other the staff."

And they answer: "Beloved lord, we shall do it."

They ride until they come to Saragossa. They go through ten gates and over four bridges and along all the streets where the townspeople live, and as they approach, at the top of the city, they hear a loud voice coming from the palace. There the pagans have assembled in great numbers, and they are weeping and moaning and showing all the signs of deep mourning. They lament the loss of Termagant and Mahomet and Apollin, their gods, which they no longer possess. And they say to each other:

"What will become of us, wretches that we are? Calamity has come upon us! We have lost King Marsiliun. Yesterday Count Roland cut off his right hand. And Jurfaret the Blond is lost to us as well. After today all of Spain will be at their mercy!"

The two messengers dismount before the steps of the palace.

CXCV

They leave their horses under an olive tree, and two Saracens take the reins. They lay hands on each other's cloaks and then go up into the lofty palace. As they enter the vaulted bedroom their fair good will leads them to utter an unfortunate greeting:

"May that Mahomet who reigns over us, and Termagant, and Apollin, our sire, protect the King and watch over the Queen!"

Bramimunde says: "What folly is this that I hear? Those gods of ours betrayed us. The miracles which they worked at Roncesvalles were disastrous! They allowed our knights to be slaughtered, and look at my lord here whom they failed in battle. He has lost his right hand. It is gone. It was cut off by that great peer Count Roland. Now Charles will rule over all of Spain and what will become of me, miserable wretch that I am? Oh alas, if only someone would kill me!"

CXCVI

Clarien says: "Lady, do not talk so much! We are messengers from the pagan Baligant, who announces that he has come to protect Marsiliun, and has sent his staff and his glove as tokens. We have four thousand vessels anchored in the Ebro, and boats and barges and galleys, and there are more transports than I can say. The Emir is rich and mighty, and is going into France to seek out Charlemagne, determined either to kill him or force him to surrender."

Bramimunde says: "It would be wrong to go so far! You will be able to find the Franks much closer to here. They have been in this country for seven years now. Their Emperor is brave and a fighter and would rather die than flee from the field. There is not a king under heaven whose strength Charles considers any more highly than that of a child, and he is not afraid of any man alive."

CXCVII

"Enough!" says King Marsiliun. To the messengers he says:

"My lords, address your words to me. As you see, the grip of death is upon me and I have neither son, nor daughter, nor heir, and the one whom I had was killed yesterday evening. Tell my lord the Emir to come and see me. He has a right to the land of Spain, and I will freely give up the kingdom in his favor, if he will have it, since he means to defend it against the French. As concerns Charlemagne, I will give him such good counsel that the Emperor will be his prisoner within the month. Take him the keys of Saragossa and tell him not to go away, if he puts any faith in my words."

They answer: "Sire, you have spoken wisely."

CXCVIII

Then Marsiliun says: "Charles the Emperor has killed my men, laid waste my kingdom, and razed and plundered my cities. Last night he camped on the banks of the Ebro, not more than seven leagues away from here, by my own count. Tell the Emir to come with his army, and in my name urge him to join battle with the Franks."

He has given them the keys of Saragossa. When he has finished speaking both of the messengers bow and take their leave.

CXCIX

Both messengers mount their horses and quickly ride out of the city, and in great agitation they come to the Emir and present him with the keys of Saragossa.

Baligant says: "What have you found out? Where is Marsiliun, whom I sent for?"

Clarien says: "He is wounded and on the point of death. Yesterday the Emperor rode into the pass intending to return to sweet France, and he left behind him a rear guard which would do him great honor. Count Roland, his nephew, remained behind there, and Oliver and all of the twelve peers, and twenty thousand armed Franks. The brave King Marsiliun attacked them; he and Roland met on the battlefield, and Roland gave him a blow with Durendal which severed his right hand. And the Count killed the King's son who was so dear to him, and the knights whom he had taken with him, and Marsiliun was unable to keep the field, and returned in full flight with the Emperor in close pursuit. The King requests your help, and in return he will freely give up the kingdom of Spain in your favor."

And Baligant falls to pondering what he has heard, and his sorrow almost deprives him of his senses.

CC

"My lord Emir," says Clarien, "there was a battle at Roncesvalles yesterday. Roland is dead, and Count Oliver, and the twelve peers who were so dear to Charles, and twenty thousand of their Franks. King Marsiliun lost his right hand, and the Emperor pursued him closely. There was not a single knight from this country who was not either killed or drowned in the Ebro. The Franks are encamped on the far shore. They have come so close to us in this country that if you chose to attack they could not get away without difficulty."

And Baligant's countenance grows proud, and his heart fills with joy and delight. From his throne he rises to his feet and calls out:

"Barons, lose no time! Descend from the ships, mount, and ride! If old Charlemagne does not flee, King Marsiliun will soon be avenged. For the loss of his right hand I will give him the Emperor's head."

CCI

The pagans from Arabia have disembarked and have mounted their horses and mules, and they ride—what more could they do? The Emir, who has wrought them up to a high pitch of excitement, summons Gemalfin, one of his favorites:

"I put all my hosts under your command."

Then he mounts his sorrel charger and with four dukes in his escort he rides to Saragossa and dismounts on a marble step with four counts holding his stirrup, and goes up the stairs into the palace. Bramimunde comes running to meet him and says to him:

"Oh miserable wretch that I am! I have lost my lord, Sire, and in a shameful manner!"

She falls at his feet and the Emir lifts her up; together, grieving, they come to the bedchamber.

CCII

When he sees Baligant, King Marsiliun calls to two Saracens of Spain:

"Take me in your arms and lift me up until I am sitting."

He has taken one of his gloves in his left hand. Then Marsiliun says:

"King, Emir, my lord, receive with this glove all my domains and Saragossa, and all the lands and titles pertaining to it. I am lost to myself and I have lost all my people."

And the other answers: "The greater is my sorrow. But I cannot stay long to talk with you, for I am sure that Charles will not wait for me. I will take your glove, though, in any case."

He turns away, weeping with grief, and descends the palace steps, mounts his horse and, digging in his spurs, rides off to rejoin his army, and at such a speed that he arrives before any of the others, and as he does so he calls out over and over:

"Come, pagans, for they are fleeing from us already!"

CCIII

In the morning, at the first light of dawn, Charles wakes, and Saint Gabriel, whom God had sent to guard him, raises one hand and blesses him with a sign. The King rises and lays aside his arms, and on all sides throughout his host his knights follow his example and disarm. Then they mount and ride at a good pace over the long highways and the broad roads until they come within sight of the terrible carnage at Roncesvalles, where the battle was.

CCIV

Charles has come to Roncesvalles, and at the sight of the dead he begins to weep. He says to the French:

"My lords, rein in your horse and ride slowly, for I must go in front and look for my nephew. It was at Aix, on a holiday, when my brave knights were boasting in my presence about great battles and furious combats, that I heard Roland describe how, if he were to die in a foreign kingdom, he would be found lying beyond his knights and his peers, on the side toward the enemy and with his head turned toward their country, and that thus the brave warrior would meet his end as a conqueror."

About as far beyond the others as one might throw a staff, the Emperor climbs a little hill.

CCV

As the Emperor goes looking for his nephew, all over the meadow he finds wild flowers which are crimson with the blood of our knights. He is overcome with pity. He weeps and cannot help it. He reaches the shade of two trees. On three stones he recognizes the strokes of Roland's sword, and then he sees his nephew lying on the grass. What wonder if Charles is torn with grief? He dismounts and runs to him, and between his two hands . . . and in his anguish he faints across the body.

CCVI

The Emperor revives, and Duke Naimes, Count Acelin, Gefrey of Anjou and his brother Henry take him up, and under a pine tree they raise him to his feet. He looks down onto the ground and sees his nephew lying there, and very tenderly he speaks his lament and farewell:

"Friend Roland, may God be merciful to you. No man ever saw such a knight as you were for forcing great battles and winning them. Now my honor has begun its decline."

Charles faints; he cannot help it.

CCVII

Charles the King recovers from his faint and four barons hold him up with their hands. He looks at the ground where his nephew is lying. The body is beautiful but it has lost all its color, and the eyes are turned upward and filled with darkness. In faith and in love Charles mourns him, saying:

"Friend Roland, may God set your soul among the flowers in Paradise, with the glorious! What an unworthy lord you followed into Spain! Not a day will pass without my grieving for you. What a falling-off there will be now in my strength and my spirit! There will be no one to maintain my honor, indeed it seems as though I had not a single friend now under heaven, and though I have kin, none of them is your equal for bravery."

With both hands he tears out his hair. A hundred thousand Franks are filled with such sorrow that there is not one of them who is not weeping.

CCVIII

"Friend Roland, I will return to France, and when I have come to Laon, to my own domain, foreign vassals will come from many kingdoms, asking:

" 'Where is your captain, the Count?'

"And I will tell them that he lies dead in Spain. And after today I will rule in great sadness, and not a day will pass but I will weep and mourn."

CCIX

"Friend Roland, brave knight, fair youth, when I have come to Aix and have entered my chapel my vassals will arrive and ask for news, and I will tell them dreadful and awesome tidings:

" 'My nephew is dead, who conquered so many countries in my name.'

"The Saxons will rebel against me, and the Hungarians, and the Bulgarians, and many other devilish races, and the Romans, and the Poles, and all those who live around Palermo, and those of Africa and those of Califerne, and my troubles and my sufferings will never leave me. Who will lead my armies with such force now that he who always rode before us is dead? Ah France, how utterly you are despoiled of men, and my own grief is such that I would rather be dead!"

He falls to tearing his beard and the hair of his head with both hands. A hundred thousand Franks faint on the ground.

CCX

"Friend Roland, may God be merciful to you and set your soul in Paradise! Whoever killed you made desolate the whole of France. And my grief for the knights of my household who have died for my sake is such that I would rather not be alive. Now, today, before I reach the great pass at Sizer, may God the son of Saint Mary be so gracious to me as to part my soul from my body and set it among their souls and give it a place there, and may my flesh be buried beside theirs."

He weeps from his eyes, he tears his white beard, and Duke Naimes says:

"Charles is in torment!"

CCXI

Then Gefrey of Anjou says: "My lord, Emperor, do not allow your-self to be so carried away with grief! Send to every part of the field and let a search be made for our men whom the Saracens of Spain killed in the battle, and have them carried to a single grave."

Then the King says: "Sound a blast on your horn."

CCXII

Gefrey of Anjou has sounded his trumpet, Charles has given the command, and the French dismount. All of their friends whom they find dead they carry to a single grave. There are many bishops and ab-bots present, and monks, canons, and tonsured priests, who absolve the dead and bless them in the name of God, and cause myrrh and incense to be kindled, and rich clouds of scented smoke to envelop the bodies, which are then buried with great honors and so left. What more could have been done?

CCXIII

The Emperor has Roland made ready for burial, and also Oliver and Archbishop Turpin. He orders all three of them to be opened in his presence, and he has their hearts brought to him, and he wraps them in silk and places them in a casket of white marble. Then the bodies of the three barons are taken and washed in wine and spices, and the lords are laid in stag skins. The King commands Tedbalt and Geboin, Count Milun and Marquis Otun:

"Let them be placed on three wagons, and you lead them."

The bodies are covered with silken palls from Galaza.

CCXIV

The Emperor is about to depart when suddenly he is confronted with the pagan vanguard. Out of their front rank ride two messengers, and in the name of their lord the Emir they announce battle:

"Haughty King, do not imagine that you will be allowed to depart. Look, here is Baligant riding behind you with the great hosts which he has brought from Arabia. Today we shall see what your courage amounts to."

Charles the King lays his hand on his beard. He calls to mind all his grief and all that he has lost. Proudly he surveys his whole army, and then in a loud ringing voice he shouts:

"Barons of France, to arms and mount!"

CCXV

The Emperor is the first to arm. Quickly he dons his coat of mail, laces on his helmet, girds on his sword Joyeuse, whose brightness even the sun does not eclipse, and around his neck he hangs a shield from Biterne. He grips his lance and brandishes it. Then he mounts his good horse Tencendur, which he had won at the ford below Marsune, hurling Malpalin of Narbonne out of the saddle, dead. He slackens the reins and spurs forward eagerly, and brings his horse to a full gallop with a hundred thousand men looking on. He calls upon God and the Apostle of Rome.

CCXVI

All over the field the French dismount, and together they arm. There are more than a hundred thousand of them, and their arms leave nothing to be desired. They have swift horses and superb weapons. They mount and go through their paces, showing their skill with their weapons, and their horsemanship. If the occasion offers they will do their part in a battle. The hanging pennons reach to their helmets.

When Charles sees the splendor of their appearance he calls to Jozeran of Provence, Duke Naimes and Antelme of Maience:

"A man can put his trust in vassals such as these, and with such knights around him only a fool could be faint-hearted. If the Arabians do not go back on their decision we will make them pay dearly for Roland's death!"

Duke Naimes answers: "God grant that we may!"

CCXVII

Charles calls to Rabel and Guinemans. Then the King says to them:

"My lords, I command you to take up Roland's position, and Oliver's. One of you carry the sword and the other the ivory horn. Ride in front, ahead of the others, and take fifteen thousand Franks with you, and let them be young, and chosen from among the bravest of your knights. And behind you will come as many more, with Geboin and Lorant leading them."

Duke Naimes and Count Jozeran form up the two battalions. If the occasion offers, the battle will be tremendous.

CCXVIII

The first two battalions of the French have been formed. They are made up of Franks from France. And after them comes the third, which is composed of some twenty thousand knights: vassals from Bavaria. The battle will not languish on their account. Except for the French themselves, who have conquered kingdoms for him, none of his followers are dearer to Charles. At their head is Count Oger the Dane, a superb fighter, for they are a proud company.

CCXIX

Charles, the Emperor, has formed three battalions. Now Duke Naimes organizes the fourth. It is made up of German barons, from

Germany, men of great courage, and their number, by common consent, is put at twenty thousand. They are well armed and well mounted, and in the face of death itself they would not give ground in a battle. Herman, the Duke of Trace, will lead them: a man who would rather die than play the coward.

CCXX

In the fifth battalion Duke Naimes and Count Jozeran have placed the Normans; according to the Frankish estimate there are twenty thousand of them, magnificently armed and mounted on fast horses. The threat of death will not make them retreat. No people under heaven can give a better account of themselves on a battlefield. Richard the Old will lead them out to the fight and will strike hard blows himself with his sharp lance.

CCXXI

The sixth battalion is made up of Bretons: a force of thirty thousand knights. There is no doubt that these are barons: you can see it as they ride out. The shafts of their lances are painted, the pennons are fixed to them. Their lord is named Oedun. He calls out to Count Nevelun, Tedbalt of Reims and Marquis Otun:
"Lead my vassals. I accord you this honor."

CCXXII

The Emperor now has six battalions ready. Duke Naimes prepares a seventh, which is made up of some forty thousand knights from Poitou and barons from the Auvergne, mounted on good horses and superbly armed. They form up in a little valley behind a hill and Charles blesses them with his right hand. Jozeran and Godselme will lead them.

CCXXIII

Duke Naimes has put the eighth battalion in order, composing it of Flemings and of Freisian barons. They number more than forty thousand knights, and the line will not falter where they hold the field. Then the King says:

"There is a company which will serve me well."

Rembalt and Hamon of Galicia will lead these fighters, and they will do it in a manner worthy of knighthood.

CCXXIV

Naimes and Count Jozeran have formed the ninth battalion, which is made up of brave vassals from Lorraine and Burgundy. They muster fifty thousand knights, with helmets laced, wearing their coats of mail, carrying stout spears with short shafts. If the Arabians do not repent their decision, these will hit them hard when they have hurled themselves into the charge. Thierry, Duke of Argonne, will lead them.

CCXXV

The tenth battalion is composed of the barons of France: one hundred thousand of our best captains, with handsome bodies and proud faces, flowing hair and white beards, wearing hauberks and double tunics of chain mail, and at their waists swords forged in France or Spain. They carry magnificent shields painted with heraldic devices. They mount. They are impatient for battle, and they raise the cry of "Mountjoy!" It is in their company that Charlemagne will ride. Gefrey of Anjou will carry the red silk banner of Saint Denis, which is the Emperor's battle flag. At one time it was Saint Peter's and was called "Rommaine," but later it too answered to the name of "Mountjoy."

CCXXVI

The Emperor dismounts and lies down on the green grass with his face turned toward the rising sun, and with all his heart he calls upon God:

"True Father, protect me today, you who delivered Jonah from the whale which had him in its body, who spared the king of Nineveh, and saved Daniel from terrible suffering when he was in the pit among the lions, and the three children in the burning oven! Keep your love close to me today, and by your grace, if it is your pleasure, grant that I may avenge my nephew Roland."

When he has made his prayer he gets to his feet and makes the sign of the cross on his brow—that sign whose powers exceed all others. Then, while Naimes and Jozeran hold the stirrup, the King mounts his swift horse and grasps his shield and his sharp lance. His body is noble and handsome, and he bears himself well. His countenance is forthright and determined. When he rides he sits his horse with assurance. The trumpets sound through the host, in the rear, in the van, and above all the others Roland's ivory horn rings out, and the Franks weep out of pity for Roland.

CCXXVII

The Emperor rides with a noble air. He has spread his beard outside his chain-mail tunic, and in their love for him all his knights do the same. Thus the hundred thousand Franks may be told apart from the others. They ride past the peaks and the rocky heights, the deep valleys, the tortuous defiles. They ride forth from the pass and the wild country and their battalions move out into Spain, where they take up positions on a stretch of open, level ground.

Baligant's scouts return to him and a Syrian delivers the message:

"We have seen Charles, the arrogant King. His men are proud; they are not of a mind to fail him. Arm, for there will be a battle, and soon."

Baligant says: "That is bravely spoken. Sound your trumpets. Let my pagans hear the news."

CCXXVIII

All through that host the drums sound, and their horns and their clear trumpets, and the pagans dismount to put on their armor. The Emir bestirs himself, not to be the last. He puts on his coat of mail with its gilt-varnished skirts, laces his helmet which is studded with jewels set in gold, and then girds his sword onto his left side. He has heard of Charles' sword, and his pride has found a name for his own: "Pre-cieuse." The word has become his battle cry; he has commanded his knights to shout "Precieuse." He hangs from his neck his great broad shield with its golden boss and crystal border; it is swung on a thick strap of silk embroidered with circles. He grasps his spear named Mal-tet, with its shaft as thick as a club. Its iron head alone would make a full load for a pack mule. Then, while Marcules, from across the sea, holds his stirrup, Baligant mounts his war horse. He has a good broad stride in the saddle, this brave knight. He is narrow in the hips, but big-ribbed, and his chest is deep and beautifully molded, his shoulders are massive, his color is fair and his face proud. His curling hair is as white as a summer flower. His courage has been proved many times. God, what a baron, if only he were a Christian! He digs his spurs into his horse until the clear blood runs. He brings it to the gallop and jumps a ditch measuring fifty feet across. The pagans cry:

"There is the man to defend the marches! Any Frenchman who dares to cross arms with him will die for it, like it or not. Charles is a fool not to have fled."

CCXXIX

You can see at a glance that the Emir is a noble baron. His beard is white as a flower. He rules with learning and wisdom, and in battle he is proud and overbearing. His son Malprimis is an ardent and accomplished knight. He is big and strong, and resembles his ancestors. He says to his father:

"Sire, now let us ride! I will be very much surprised if we see Charles at all."

Baligant says: "We will see him, for he is a very brave man. There are many stories about him which redound to his great honor. But his nephew Roland is no longer with him, and he will not be able to hold the field against us."

CCXXX

Then Baligant says: "Fair son Malprimis, yesterday Roland, that good vassal, was killed, and so was brave noble Oliver, and so were the twelve peers who were so dear to Charles, and so were twenty thousand warriors of France. As for all the others, I would not give a glove for them. It is true, the Emperor has returned: my messenger, the Syrian, has brought me word. Charles has ten huge battalions. Someone is sounding Roland's ivory horn. He is a brave man. And his companions give answer with the clear note of a trumpet, and those two ride out ahead of the others, and fifteen thousand Franks with them, knights in the first strength of their youth, whom Charles calls his sons. Behind them come the same number again. They will attack with pride."

Malprimis says: "Grant me the first blow."

CCXXXI

Baligant says to him: "My son, Malprimis, I grant what you ask. Ride to attack the French, and take with you Torleu, the Persian King, and Dapamort, the King of Lycia. If you can smash the towering pride of the first battalions, I will give you a piece of my own domain, from Cheriant to Val Marchis."

The other answers: "Sire, receive my thanks!"

He advances and accepts the gift: a piece of land which had once belonged to King Flurit. As for Malprimis, it did not bring him luck, for he never set eyes on it. It never became his, and he was never its lord.

CCXXXII

The Emir rides through that host, with his tall son behind him. King Torleu and King Dapamort form up thirty battalions at once, filling them with vast numbers of men: in the smallest of those companies there are fifty thousand knights. The first is made up of warriors from Butentrot; the one which follows it is composed of vassals from Micenes, with big heads. Like hogs, they have bristles all along their spines. And the third battalion contains the vassals from Nubles and Blos, and the fourth those from Bruns and Esclavons, and the fifth those from Sobres and Sores, and the sixth the Armenians and the Moors, the seventh the knights from Jericho, the eighth those from Nigres, the ninth those from Gros, and the tenth is made up of vassals from the stronghold of Balide, whose people have always been a race of malefactors. The Emir swears by all that he holds sacred, by the miracles and body of Mahomet:

"Charles is a fool to ride against us! Unless he breaks and runs now, there will be a battle and he will never again wear a golden crown."

CCXXXIII

Then they assembled another ten battalions. The first musters the ugly men of Canaan, who have come by way of Val Fuit, crossing it from one side to the other. Next comes the battalion of Turks. And third, the Persians. And the fourth is composed of Pincenians and . . . and the fifth of Solterans and Avars, and the sixth of Ormalians and Eugles, and the seventh of the people of Samuel, and the eighth of the vassals from Brusse, and the ninth of the vassals from Clavers, and the tenth is made up of those who come from the desert of Occian, a people who do not serve the Lord God, and as villainous a race as you will ever hear mentioned. Their skins are as hard as iron, so that they do not need either helmet or hauberk, and they are brutal and headstrong in battle.

CCXXXIV

The Emir has drawn up another ten battalions. In the first of them are the giants from Malprose, in the second the Huns, in the third the Hungarians, and in the fourth are the vassals from Long Baldisa, and in the fifth those from Val Penuse, and in the sixth those from . . . Maruse, and in the seventh those from Leus and Astrimonia. The eighth is made up of warriors from Argoilles, and the ninth of those from Clarbone, and in the tenth are assembled the long-bearded knights from Fronde, a race which never love God. And thus, according to the Chronicle of the Franks, they mustered thirty battalions. From one end of that enormous host to the other the trumpets sound, and the pagans ride out bravely.

CCXXXV

The Emir has vast powers at his command. He sends his standard bearers before him with his dragon and the banner of Termagant and Mahomet, and an image of the villain Apollin. Ten Canaanites ride with the banners, chanting in loud voices:

"Let every one who hopes for the protection of our gods pray to them now and cast himself down in their worship!"

The pagans bow their heads and their chins to them, and incline their shining helmets.

The French say: "Base wretches, you are close to death! May utter destruction overwhelm you today! Oh Lord Our God, defend Charles, and in his name may this battle be . . .

CCXXXVI

The Emir is a man of great wisdom. He calls to his son and the two kings:

"Barons, my lords, ride before us and lead all my battalions except three of the best which I shall keep with me: the first of them made up of Turks, the next of Ormalians, and the third of the Malprosian giants. And the knights from Occian will go with me and fight against Charles and the French. If the Emperor contests the field with me he will lose the head from his shoulders. It will be done, and that will be all, and that will end his claims."

CCXXXVII

Huge are the hosts and beautiful their battalions, and between the two armies there is neither mountain nor valley nor hill nor forest nor wood. Nothing and no one can be hidden; they are all in plain sight, with open country around them.

Baligant says: "Pagans, my vassals, ride forward now and join battle."

Amborres of Oluferne carries his standard, and the pagans raise the battle cry of "Precieuse!"

The French say: "May your losses be heavy today!" and with loud voices they renew the shout of "Mountjoy!" The Emperor gives the command for his trumpets to sound, and with them Roland's ivory horn, which rings out above all the others.

The pagans say: "Charles has a magnificent army. Our battle will be fierce and bitter."

CCXXXVIII

They are on a broad plain, in open country, and their helmets studded with jewels set in gold, and their shields and their gilt-varnished tunics of chain mail and their spears and the banners fixed to them are all shining. The trumpets sound, raising their clear voices. The high note of Roland's ivory horn sounds the charge. The Emir calls to his brother, Canabeus, the King of Floredee, whose domain extends as far as Val Sevree, and shows him Charles' battalions.

"Look! There is the pride of famous France, and there is the Emperor riding boldly. He is toward the rear, among those knights who have let their long snow-white beards flow loose over their tunics of chain mail. They will strike with lances and with swords, and the battle between us will be so fierce and furious that no man will ever have seen the like."

Baligant rides on ahead of his knights until he is a little farther in front of them than a man might throw a peeled wand, and then he calls out:

"Come, pagans, for I am on my way!"

He brandishes the shaft of his spear, and then he turns the point toward Charles.

CCXXXIX

When Charles the Great sees the Emir and the dragon and the banner and the standard, and when he sees the host of the Arabians and how vast it is, spreading over the countryside everywhere except where the Emperor's own army is waiting, the King of France calls in a loud voice:

"Barons of France, you are good vassals and you have fought many battles in the field. You can see the pagans: they are evil and cowardly and their whole credo will not do them a farthing's worth of good. What difference does it make, my lords, if they come in great numbers? If any man does not wish to come with me let him go now!"

Then he spurs his horse, Tencendur, which bounds forward in four great leaps.

The French say: "Here is a noble king! Ride, brave knights! Not one of us will fail you!"

CCXL

The day was clear and the sun was bright. Beautiful are the hosts and huge their battalions, and the first ranks of the two armies are face to face. Count Rabel and Count Guinemans give rein to their fast horses and spur forward, and with that the French charge, hurling themselves forward to strike with their sharp spears.

CCXLI

Count Rabel, that bold knight, digs in his spurs of pure gold and rides to attack Torleu, the Persian king. Neither shield nor chain mail withstand the blow, but the gilded spearshaft drives through the pagan's body and the corpse is flung down onto a little bush.

The French say: "May the Lord God be our help! Charles is in the right. We must not fail him."

CCXLII

And Guinemans charges at the King of Lycia and smashes his shield painted with flowers, and he bursts the pagan's chain-mail tunic and buries the whole of his pennon in the other's body, killing him, let men mourn or laugh as they will. At the sight of that blow the French shout:

"Strike, baron, and do not spare! Charles is in the right, fighting against these . . . God has chosen us to be instruments of His true justice."

CCXLIII

Malprimis, mounted on a pure white horse, hurls himself into the thick of the Frankish host, dealing hard blows first on one side, then on another, and flinging corpse upon corpse without pausing. Before any of the others raises his voice, Baligant shouts:

"My barons, for a long time I have fed you at my table. Look: my son is making his way toward Charles, wielding his arms in defiance of so many knights. I could not ask for a better vassal. To his help now with your sharp spears!"

At this word the pagans advance. They strike hard blows. There is vast slaughter. The battle is crushing and awesome, and such a struggle has never been seen before or since.

CCXLIV

Huge are the hosts and fierce are their companies, and by now all of the battalions on both sides have met, and the pagans strike hard. Oh God, there are so many spear shafts splintered, shields smashed and mailed tunics burst apart! The ground is littered with them, and the green tender grass of the field. The Emir calls out to his vassals:

"Strike, barons, against the Christian host!"

The battle is furious, with neither side giving ground. Never before nor since has there been a struggle like this one. It will go on without a pause until nightfall.

CCXLV

The Emir calls to his knights:

"Strike, pagans! That is what you came for! I will give you noble and lovely wives, and I will give you domains and honors and lands!"

The pagans answer: "It is our duty to obey."

With the shock of heavy blows, spear after spear has splintered, and then over a hundred thousand swords are drawn. Now the slaughter becomes grim and terrible, and any man who is in the midst of that fighting learns what a battle is.

CCXLVI

The Emperor calls out to the French:

"Barons, my lords, my love for you is great, and I have faith in you. You have fought so many battles for me, you have conquered so many kingdoms and dethroned so many kings. I have not forgotten that the reward I owe you is nothing less than myself: body, lands, and possessions. Avenge your sons, your brothers, your heirs who were killed the other evening at Roncesvalles! You know that I am in the right, fighting against the pagans."

The Franks answer: "Sire, what you say is true."

And twenty thousand of those who are closest to him pronounce a solemn oath together, swearing that they will not fail him though they are faced with death or pain. Every one of them puts his spear to good use, and then they strike with their swords, and the battle grows bloody and awesome.

CCXLVII

And Malprimis rides over the field inflicting terrible slaughter on the Franks, until Duke Naimes turns a proud glance upon him and rides bravely to attack him. The Duke smashes through the top part of the pagan's shield and cleaves through both thicknesses of his double hauberk, burying the whole of his spear to the end of its yellow pennon in the other's body and hurling down his corpse among seven hundred others.

CCXLVIII

King Canabeus, the Emir's brother, digs his spurs into his horse. He has drawn his crystal-pointed sword, and with it he strikes Naimes on the top of the helmet, which splits apart into two pieces. His steel blade cuts through five of the helmet laces and, slicing through the hood of chain mail as though it were nothing, parts the cap, comes to the flesh and hacks off a piece, which is hurled to the ground. The Duke is stunned by the heavy blow, and is about to fall, when God helps him, and he grips the neck of his horse with both arms. If the pagan can rein up and return once more the noble vassal will be killed. But Charles of France comes to his aid.

CCXLIX

Duke Naimes is in great distress, and the pagan rushes to strike him again. Charles says:

"Base wretch, that blow will call down sorrow upon you!"

And the Emperor rides bravely to strike him, and breaks his shield, crushing it against his heart, and smashes the lower part of his helmet, and hurls his corpse to the ground, leaving the saddle empty.

CCL

Charlemagne the King, when he sees Duke Naimes wounded before his eyes and the bright blood falling onto the green grass, is filled with bitter grief. The Emperor says to him:

"Naimes, fair sir, ride along beside me. That base creature who was about to attack you in your distress is dead now. This time I ran my spear through his body."

The Duke answers: "Sire, I put my trust in you. If I survive this, your help to me will be rewarded."

Then in love and in faith they ride along together, and with them twenty thousand of the French, every one of them cleaving and hacking as he goes.

CCLI

The Emir rides over the field and charges to attack Count Guinemans, smashing his white shield against his breast, bursting the folds of his hauberk, splitting his chest in two and hurling him, dead, from his running horse. After that he kills Geboin and Lorant, and Richard the Old, the lord of the Normans.

The pagans shout: "Brave Precieuse! Strike, barons, for our defense is with us!"

CCLII

Then what a sight to see the warriors of Arabia and the ones from Occian and from Argoille and Bascle, striking and thrusting with their spears! The French are not tempted to flee; many die on the one side and on the other, and the battle rages in full fury into the evening. Great numbers of the Frankish barons are killed. The grief will be worse before it is over.

CCLIII

Both the French and the Arabians fight hard, and their shafts and polished lances are snapped. And if you had been there what a sight you would have seen of smashed shields, and what a din you would have heard of hauberks hacked apart and of shields grating against helmets. You would have seen knights falling, and men howling and dying on the ground, and you would have brought away a memory of great suffering! It is a harsh and terrible battle to live through. The Emir calls upon Apollin and upon Termagant and Mahomet as well:

"My lord, my god, I have served you for many years. Now I will have your images made of pure gold ..."

Gemalfin, one of his favorites, appears before him bearing bad news, and says:

"Baligant, sire, sorrow has come to you. You have lost Malprimis, your son, and Canabeus, your brother, has been killed. Two of the French have been lucky and have struck them down, and one of the two, I believe, was the Emperor. He was large of stature, and his bearing was that of a ruler, and his beard was as white as a flower in April."

The Emir bows his helmet, and after that his face darkens. His grief is so terrible that it seems as though he were dying. Then he calls to Jangleu from Outremer.

CCLIV

The Emir says: "Jangleu, come before me. You are a brave knight, and very wise, and I have always ... heeded your counsel. What do you think of the Arabians and the Franks: will victory be ours on this field?"

And the other answers: "Baligant, you are a dead man! Your gods will not protect you. Charles is proud, and his men are brave, and never have I seen an army fight as this one is fighting. But call up the barons from Occian, and the Turks and Enfruns, the Arabs and the Giants. What is fated will happen, but do not waste time in waiting."

CCLV

The Emir has spread his beard out over his chest, and it is as white as any thorn flower: whatever happens he does not want to be hidden. He sets his clear-voiced trumpet to his mouth and blows a ringing blast so that all his pagans may hear it, and from all over the field his vassals rally to him. Those who have come from Occian bray and whinny, and those from Argoille yelp like dogs, and they hurl themselves recklessly into the thick of the Franks and break and scatter them, in this one charge flinging down seven thousand dead.

CCLVI

Count Oger was never a coward, and no better knight ever wore a coat of mail. When he sees the French battalions scattered he calls to Thierry, the Duke of Argonne, and to Gefrey of Anjou and Count Jozeran, and with great pride he addresses Charles:

"See how the pagans are slaughtering your men! May it grieve God to see the crown on your head if you do not strike now to avenge your shame!"

No one says a word in reply to this, but they all dig in their spurs and give rein to their horses and ride to attack the pagans wherever they may find them.

CCLVII

Charlemagne the King strikes hard and well, and so does Duke Naimes, and so do Oger the Dane and Gefrey of Anjou, who carries the standard. And the bravery of Oger the Dane is without peer. He spurs his horse, gives it full rein, and strikes Amborres, the pagan standard-bearer, with such force that the other is hurled to the ground head first, and with him the dragon and the pagan King's ensign. Baligant sees his pennon fall and the standard of Mahomet struck down, and at that moment the Emir perceives that he is in the wrong, and that Charlemagne is in the right. The pagans from Arabia give ground ...

The Emperor calls out to the French: "Tell me, my barons, in the name of God will you lend me your help now?"

The French answer: "What is the good of asking? A curse on any man who does not strike with all his heart!"

CCLVIII

The day passes, the evening comes, and Franks and pagans fight on with their swords. Those who have led these two hosts into battle are brave men. They have not forgotten their war-cries: the Emir shouts, "Precieuse!" and Charles raises his famous battle cry of "Mountjoy!" And by their clear ringing voices the two men recognize each other, and they meet in the middle of the field and ride to attack each other, and exchange heavy blows, each one's spear smashing into the other's ringed shield. And each shield is pierced above the broad boss, and the folds of both of their hauberks are rent, but on neither side do the spears enter the flesh. Their cinches break and their saddles tip over and both kings fall to the ground, but they leap to their feet at once and bravely draw their swords. Now nothing can separate them, and the fight cannot end except with the death of one or the other.

CCLIX

Charles of sweet France is gifted with great courage, and the Emir shows neither dread nor hesitation. They draw their swords, showing the naked blades, and they deal each other heavy blows on their shields, cutting through the leather coverings and the two outer layers of wood, so that the nails fall and the buckles are broken in pieces. Then, bare of shields, they hack at each other's coats of mail, and the sparks leap from their bright helmets. This combat cannot be brought to an end without one or the other confessing that he is in the wrong.

CCLX

The Emir says: "Charles, consider the matter carefully and make up your mind to repent for what you have done to me. You have killed my son, if I am not mistaken, and you are wrongfully disputing with me the possession of my own country. If you will become my vassal [and swear fealty to me] you may come with me and serve me from here to the East."

Charles answers: "To my way of thinking that would be vile and base. It is not for me to render either peace or love to a pagan. Submit to the creed which God has revealed to us, become a Christian, and my love for you will never end as long as you put your faith in the omnipotent King and serve Him."

Baligant says: "You have begun a bad sermon!" Then they raise their swords and resume the fight.

CCLXI

The Emir is a strong and skillful fighter. He strikes Charlemagne upon his helmet of burnished steel and splits and smashes it above his head, bringing the sword down into the fine hair, sheering off a palm's breadth and more of flesh, and laying bare the bone. Charles staggers and almost falls, but it is not God's will that he should be killed or beaten. Saint Gabriel comes to his side, asking:

"Great King, what are you doing?"

CCLXII

When he hears the holy voice of the angel, Charles loses all fear of death, and his vigor and clearness of mind return. He strikes the Emir a blow with the sword of France, cleaves the helmet flashing with jewels, cuts open the head and spills the brains, and splits the whole face down through the white beard. It is a corpse, past all hope of recovery, which that stroke hurls to the ground. Charles calls "Mountjoy!" to rally his vassals, and at his shout Duke Naimes comes to him bringing with him the Emperor's horse Tencendur, and the King mounts.

The pagans flee. It is not the will of God that they should remain. Now the French have achieved the triumph which they had hoped for.

CCLXIII

The pagans flee, for such is the will of the Lord God, and the Franks, and the Emperor with them, give chase. Then the King says:

"Now, my lords, avenge your griefs. Show your wills now and the passions of your hearts, for this morning I saw the tears running from your eyes."

The Franks answer: "Sire, we must do so."

And each of them strikes blow after heavy blow, with all his heart, and of the pagans who are there, few escape.

CCLXIV

In the fierce heat the dust rises. The pagans flee; the French harry them, and the pursuit continues as far as Saragossa.

Bramimunde has climbed to the top of her tower. She has with her there her clerics and canons of the false religion which God never loved. They have not been ordained and their heads are not tonsured. When she sees the rout of the Arabians she calls out in a loud voice:

"Help us, Mahomet! Ah noble King, our men have been beaten, and the Emir has been killed, to add to the shame of it!"

When Marsiliun hears her he turns to the wall with the tears running from his eyes, his head sinks, and he dies of sorrow with the weight of his sin upon him. His soul is given to the quick demons.

CCLXV

The pagans are dead. Many of them ... And Charles has won his battle. He has beaten down the gate of Saragossa and he knows beyond any doubt that it will not be defended. He occupies the city. His army enters its walls. His men lodge there that night by right of conquest. The white-bearded King is filled with pride, for Bramimunde has surrendered her towers to him—the ten enormous ones and the fifty smaller ones.

He whom the Lord God helps will triumph.

CCLXVI

The day passes. The night has grown dark. The moon is bright and the stars shine. The Emperor has taken Saragossa.

He sends a thousand French, bearing hammers and iron mallets, to search through the city's mosques and synagogues and to smash the images and all the idols, sparing nothing which pertains to the black arts and false creeds of the heathen. Because the King believes in God, he is eager to serve Him, and his bishops bless water, and the pagans are led into the baptistry. If anyone resists Charles, he is hanged or burned or put to the sword, and more than a hundred thousand of them are baptized and become true Christians. But not the Queen. She is to be led captive into sweet France, where the King hopes that she will be converted by love.

CCLXVII

The night passes and the bright day appears. Charles garrisons the towers of Saragossa, leaving a thousand intrepid knights to guard the city in the Emperor's name. The King and all his men mount their horses, and Bramimunde with them, whom he is taking in his company, a prisoner, though it is not his will that anything except good should befall her. Rejoicing and triumphant, they return toward

France. In their strength and vigor they seize Narbonne and pass on, and reach Bordeaux, the city . . . On noble Saint Seurin's altar he lays Roland's ivory horn filled with gold and with gold pieces; the pilgrims who go there can see it still. He and his army enter into the great ships which are there and cross the Gironde. As far as Blaye he carries his nephew's body, and the body of his noble companion Oliver, and the body of the wise and brave Archbishop. There he commands them to enclose the three lords in white sarcophagi, and they are lying there still at Saint-Romain, those noble knights. The French commend them to God and to His holy name.

After that, Charles rides through the valleys and over the mountains, refusing to break his journey until he has come to Aix, and at last he dismounts on his own threshold. And when he has entered the royal palace he sends messengers to summon his judges, Bavarians and Saxons, and those from Lorraine and Freisia. He sends to the Germans, he sends to the Burgundians, and to the Poitevins and the Normans and the Bretons, and to the judges of France, whose wisdom is unsurpassed. Then the trial of Ganelon begins.

CCLXVIII

The Emperor has returned from Spain and has come to Aix, which is without peer among the seats of France. He climbs the steps and goes into his palace and enters the hall. Now Alde, a beautiful girl, approaches him, and she says to the King:

"Where is Roland, the captain, who swore that he would take me to be his wife?"

Charles is filled with sorrow and grief. The tears run from his eyes and he rends his white beard.

"Sister, beloved friend, you are asking for a dead man. In his place I will give you a vassal who is even more nobly born than Roland was, and that is Louis, and better than that I cannot say. He is my son, and it is he who will rule my marches."

Alde answers: "Your words are strange to me. May it not please God nor His saints nor His angels that I should continue to live when Roland is dead!"

The color drains from her face, and she falls at Charlemagne's feet and dies. May God have mercy on her soul! The French barons weep and mourn for her.

CCLXIX

Alde the Lovely is no longer alive. And the King pities her, thinking that she has fainted; the Emperor weeps for her and takes her by the hand and draws her up. Her head falls onto her shoulders. When Charles sees that she is dead he sends at once and summons four countesses, and they bear Alde's body to a nuns' convent. There a watch is kept over her all night and into the dawn. Then, beside an altar, she is buried with great ceremony, and the King accords her many honors.

CCLXX

The Emperor has returned to Aix. Ganelon, the villain, is brought in iron chains into the city, and taken before the palace, where the serfs bind him to a stake, tying his hands with deer-hide thongs. Then they beat him soundly with wooden clubs and cudgels. Certainly he has earned no better reward. And there in great pain he awaits his trial.

CCLXXI

It is written in the old story that Charles sent into many lands to summon his vassals. They have assembled at Aix, in his chapel. It is a holiday, an occasion of high solemnity—many say that it is noble Saint Sylvester's day. Then the trial and the giving of evidence concerning Ganelon, the traitor, begin. The Emperor has the man dragged before him.

CCLXXII

"Barons, my lords," says King Charlemagne, "consider the rights of the case and judge Ganelon for me. He came with me into Spain in the army, and his presence cost me twenty thousand of my French knights, and my nephew, whom you will never see again, and brave, courteous Oliver, and he betrayed the twelve peers for gain."

Ganelon says: "I would be ashamed to deny what I have done! Because of Roland I had lost gold and possessions, and it was for that reason that I set about to cause his death and his ruin. But as for treachery, I will not admit to anything of the kind."

The French answer: "We will deliberate upon the matter."

CCLXXIII

There stands Ganelon, before the King. His body is handsome, his color is fresh and fair, and if only he had been loyal his appearance would be in every respect that of a noble knight. He looks at the French vassals and at all his judges, and at the thirty members of his own family who are there on his account, and then he calls out in a loud voice:

"Barons, for the love of God listen to me! My lords, I was in the host with the Emperor and I served him in faith and in love. His nephew Roland conceived a hatred for me and contrived my death and sorrow. I was sent as an envoy to King Marsiliun, and nothing but my own wit saved me. I challenged Roland, that fearless and skillful fighter, and I challenged Oliver and all their companions. Charles and his noble barons heard me. And I have avenged myself, but there has been no treachery."

The French answer: "We must put it to debate."

CCLXXIV

When Ganelon sees that the great trial is about to begin there are thirty of his relatives there with him. Pinabel, from the castle of

Sorence, is the spokesman for the rest, for he is an eloquent and persuasive speaker, and a brave knight when it comes to trials of arms. Then Ganelon says to him:

"In you ... friend ... Now save me from death and calumny!"

Pinabel says: "You will be saved, and it will not take long. No Frank will condemn you to be hanged, or if he does the Emperor will set our two bodies in the lists together and I will give him the lie with my steel blade."

Count Ganelon bows down at his feet.

CCLXXV

The Bavarians and the Saxons have entered into council, and the Poitevins and the Normans and the French. There are many Germans and Teutons there, and the vassals from the Auvergne are the most courteous of all. They all speak more softly, because of Pinabel. One says to another:

"It would be best to leave things as they are. Let us abandon the trial and ask the King to allow Ganelon to go free this time. Then let him serve the Emperor with love and faith in the future. Roland is dead; you will never see him again, and no gold and no riches will bring him back. Any man who ... would put it to the combat is a fool many times over."

And everyone agrees except Thierry, Gefrey's brother.

CCLXXVI

The barons return to Charlemagne and say to the King: "Sire, we beg you to acquit Count Ganelon of this charge. Let him serve you with love and faith in the future. Grant him his life, for he comes of a noble line. Besides, his death will not bring Roland back to you, nor will any riches restore your nephew."

Then the King says: "You are despicable villains."

CCLXXVII

When Charles sees that they have all failed him, he bows his head and his face in grief, and in his sorrow he cries out:

"Alas, what a wretch I am!"

It is then that a knight named Thierry, the brother of the Angevin Duke Gefrey, stands up before the King. He is gaunt of limb, and wiry, and quick, with black hair, and his face is swarthy. He is neither very tall nor very short. In a courteous manner he says to the Emperor:

"Fair sire, King, do not thus abandon yourself to despair! You know that I have served you long and well, and I owe it to the honor of my ancestors to uphold your accusation. However Ganelon may have had cause to complain of Roland, Roland was your officer, which in itself should have rendered him inviolable. And Ganelon is a villain for having betrayed him and for having lied to you and for having broken his oath to you. Therefore I condemn him to be hanged until he is dead, and his body put . . . like any common criminal. If any of his kin wish to contest what I say I will defend my judgment at once with this sword which I have girded to my side."

The Franks answer: "Now you have spoken well."

CCLXXVIII

Pinabel has come to stand before the King. He is tall and strong and brave and quick, and if he strikes a man a blow, the other has come to the end of his days. He says to the King:

"Sire, this is your trial. Command them to make less noise! With regard to Thierry, here, who has pronounced judgment, I declare his sentence to be false, and I will fight him."

He hands the King the deer-skin glove from his right hand. The Emperor says:

"I must have sufficient pledges."

Thirty of Ganelon's relatives offer themselves as loyal hostages. Then the King says:

"You may go free while these stand surety for you."

And he has the hostages put under guard until justice is done.

CCLXXIX

When Thierry sees that there will be a trial by arms, he gives Charles his right glove, and the Emperor himself stands surety for him and allows him his freedom. Then the King has four benches brought into the place and those who are to fight go and sit there. All who are present agree that the challenge has been given and accepted according to the rules. Oger of Denmark repeats the words of defiance in the names of both parties. Then the combatants send for their horses and their arms.

CCLXXX

When they have got ready for the combat they make confession and receive absolution and a benediction, and hear mass and take communion. Each of them makes a large offering to his church. Then both of them come before Charles.

They have put their spurs on their feet and donned their strong, light, shining hauberks, and laced their helmets onto their heads. They have girded on their gold-hilted swords and hung their shields, with the quarterings painted on them, around their necks. They take their sharp spears in their right hands. Then they mount their swift horses.

As they do, a hundred thousand knights fall to weeping, in pity for Roland and Thierry.

God knows how the fight will end.

CCLXXXI

Below the city of Aix there is a broad meadow, and there the two barons come together to fight. Both of them are noble and courageous, and their horses are swift and high-spirited. They dig in their spurs and loosen the reins all the way, and with all their might they charge at each other. Their shields are shattered and smashed, their hauberks are rent. And the cinches are burst so that the saddlebows are overturned and the saddles fall to the ground.

A hundred thousand men weep as they watch them.

CCLXXXII

Both knights have fallen to the ground, but they leap to their feet at once. Pinabel is strong and light and quick. They rush at each other on foot, and with their gold-hilted swords they hew and hack at each other's steel helmets. The blows are heavy, and the helmets are gashed and rent. And the French knights raise loud laments.

"Oh God," says Charles, "reveal the right!"

CCLXXXIII

Pinabel says: "Thierry, admit yourself beaten! I will become your vassal in all love and faith, and will give you as much of my wealth as you please, but make peace between Ganelon and the King!"

Thierry answers: "I will not long debate the matter. May the name of a villain belong to me many times over if I agree to the smallest detail of what you ask. And may God this day show which of us is in the right!"

CCLXXXIV

Then Thierry says: "Pinabel, you are noble and knightly, you are tall and strong, your body is well molded, and your peers are in no doubt as to your courage. Abandon this fight now. I will make peace between you and Charlemagne. But Ganelon will have justice meted out to him, and in such a manner that a day will never pass without its being retold."

Pinabel says: "The Lord God forbid! I will uphold the honor of my family, and I will not yield for any mortal man. I would rather die than suffer disgrace."

They raise their swords again and strike each other on the helmets which are studded with jewels set in gold, and the bright sparks fly up toward heaven. Now there is nothing that can separate them, and the fight cannot end without the death of one or the other.

CCLXXXV

Pinabel of Sorence is strong and fearless. He strikes Thierry on the helmet, which comes from Provence, and the sparks leap and set fire to the grass. Then he lunges with the point of his sword and strikes Thierry a blow on the forehead [and cuts off] a piece of his face, leaving the right cheek streaming blood, and covering Thierry's hauberk with blood as far down as the waist. God alone saves him from being killed on the spot.

CCLXXXVI

Thierry sees that he has been wounded in the face, and that his bright blood is falling onto the grass of the meadow. He strikes Pinabel on the burnished steel helmet and splits it down as far as the nose piece, spilling the brains out of the head. Then he wrenches the blade in the wound and hurls down his opponent, dead. With that blow he has won the fight.

The French shout: "God has wrought a miracle! Justice demands that Ganelon should be hanged, and with him his kinfolk, who took his part."

CCLXXXVII

When Thierry has won his battle the Emperor Charles comes to his side, and four of his barons come with him: Duke Naimes, Oger of Denmark, Gefrey of Anjou, and William of Blaye. The King embraces Thierry, and wipes Thierry's face with his great sable mantle. Then he lays that mantle aside and puts on another. Very gently the knight is disarmed, and they mount him on a mule from Arabia. And they return, celebrating and rejoicing, and come to Aix, and dismount in the square.

Then the execution of the others begins.

CCLXXXVIII

Charles summons his counts and his dukes.

"What do you suggest that I should do with those whom I have under guard? They came here to maintain Ganelon's case, and they gave themselves up to me as hostages for Pinabel."

The Franks answer: "It would be wrong to spare the life of a single one of them."

The King sends for one of his officers, named Basbrun:

"Go and hang all of them on the malefactors' tree, and by this white beard I will see you dead and cursed to damnation if any one of them is allowed to escape."

The other answers: "I have no choice but to obey." He takes a hundred sergeants and drags the condemned men by main force to the place of execution. There are thirty of them who are hanged. The traitor brings death upon himself and upon others.

CCLXXXIX

And after this the Bavarians and the Germans and the Poitevins and the Bretons and the Normans, but first and most particularly the Franks, agree that Ganelon should be executed in some terrible and painful manner. They bring four war horses, and to them they tie Ganelon's feet and hands. They are proud, swift horses. Four sergeants urge them on toward a stream in the middle of a field. Ganelon comes to a terrible end. All his nerves are distended and every limb of his body is broken. His bright blood streams out over the green grass. Ganelon dies like a wretched felon. If a man is a traitor, it is not right that he should live to boast of it.

CCXC

When the Emperor has taken his vengeance he summons to him the bishops of France, Bavaria and Germany:

"There is a noble prisoner in my house who has heard so many sermons and parables that she has come to believe in God and has asked to be made a Christian. Baptize her, so that God may receive her soul."

They answer him: "Let her be provided with godmothers."

. . . .

In the baths at Aix there are great . . . There they baptize the Queen of Spain, giving her the name of Julienne, which they have chosen for her, and by virtue of her true knowledge of the faith she is made a Christian.

CCXCI

When the Emperor has meted out his justice and satisfied his great wrath and has had Bramimunde baptized a Christian, the day is over and the night has darkened.

The King has gone to bed in his vaulted bedroom. God sends Saint Gabriel to him, to say to him:

"Charles, summon all the hosts of your Empire and enter the land of Bire by force of arms, and rescue King Vivien, for the pagans have laid siege to him in the city of Imphe, and the Christians there are pleading and crying out for you."

The Emperor does not wish to go.

"Oh God," says the King, "my life is a burden!" And the tears run from his eyes and he rends his white beard.

The story which Toruldus set down ends here.

AFTERWORD

by M. A. Clermont-Ferrand

Life in medieval Europe was often full of disease, poverty, and violence, yet the Middle Ages can also be described as a time of spectacular beauty. It was the age of soaring cathedrals, of poignant polyphonic chants, and of a thriving literature peopled with brave heroes who dedicated their lives to causes larger than themselves. The poet-composer of *La Chanson de Roland* preserved that world for us. His poetry shows us the mores, rules, and promises that governed a knight of the poem's Carolingian Empire. A knight vowed to remain faithful to his liege lord, to honor his word, to fight his lord's enemies, and die in battle if necessary.

What encouraged a man to hold firm to the vows he took? The answer that relates most directly to *Roland* is the concept of *preu d'homme,* an Old French term that means a knight's reputation after his death. A knight knew that his life would likely be violent and short. Therefore, he spent his martial career trying to establish a reputation for bravery, honor, and loyalty so that his name at least would live on in the songs sung in remembrance of him.

Roland, a *chanson de geste* that celebrates a Christian victory over the Muslims of Spain, evolved from a type of tenth-century Arabic song, the *qasida,*[1] that was popular in Andalusia, the province at the heart of Muslim-controlled Spain. The *qasida* was a long poem constructed around rhyming vowel sounds, much like the assonance in the original French of *Roland.* The Arab poets ingeniously wrote poems around one rhyme, so successfully that sometimes a composition could extend to over one hundred lines.[2] The *qasida* was used to immortalize and glorify men who had accomplished great military exploits.

The writers of the provinces of southern France, where the main action of *Roland* takes place, were influenced by the Andalusian Arabic poetic conventions as in no other part of western Europe. Arabic poetry in Andalusia was sung with musical accompaniment, unlike that of the eastern Muslim provinces, where poetry was sung a cappella. Some medieval scholars hypothesize that in addition to borrowing the *qasida* as a form of poetry, French poets also borrowed the musical instruments.[3] So even though the author of *Roland* used his work to glorify men who fought the Muslims in Spain, he did so in a form borrowed from Muslim tradition.

The French singers and poets who modified the *qasida* and immortalized the knights such as Roland were called jongleurs. Though they sometimes had patrons, often they were itinerant musicians and poets who made their living by wandering from place to place and playing.

From what we can recover of the art of the jongleurs, they spoke of knights as the building blocks of the early nation. They gave their audiences ideals of men whose superhuman bravery, loyalty, and feats of strength both inspired other men to the same high ideals and ensured the immortality of their long-dead subjects. Thus jongleurs shaped the mores and aspirations of the knightly and governing classes for centuries.

Christianity promised another kind of eternal life. If a knight spent his life in service of the church, he was guaranteed an eternity in paradise. And this Christian thinking was deeply embedded in both the knight's vows and his assessments of his military goals. Such thinking also ensured that the church's more worldly and political ideas were well supported by force. When a knight took his oath and promised to defend his liege lord, to honor his word and to fight bravely even at the cost of his own life, he also promised to honor God and to defend the Christian church.

Roland's faithfulness to the Holy Roman Emperor Charlemagne is unmistakable. Turning to what is called the poem's first horn scene, *laisses* LXXXIII through LXXXVII, Oliver, Roland's friend and fighting companion, has seen that the Muslim army outnumbers them and begs Roland to sound his ivory horn to bring Charlemagne and the Carolingian army to their aid. But Roland feels that calling for help would shame him and France.

> "God forbid that any man living should be able to say that because of the pagans I blew my ivory horn! No one will ever be able to shame my family with the mention of such a thing.... The French are brave, they will fight hard and well, and those who come from Spain will not be saved from death.... For the sake of his lord a man must be prepared to sacrifice even his blood and his flesh."

Roland's honor required him to live up to his promise to Charlemagne that he would make the Muslims pay for any assault on the Frankish forces.

The Holy Roman Empire, the bulk of territory that swore loyalty to the

Pope, belonged to Roland's overlord, Charlemagne. Unity of the Christian West was imperative if the Muslims were to be driven out of Spain. The Charlemagne of *La Chanson de Roland* as well as the historical Charlemagne worked tirelessly to uphold his *preu d'homme* and wage war in the name of religious *reconquistor* as well as political conqueror. Charlemagne spent the majority of his reign trying to subdue and Christianize neighboring regions.

In 778, the year of the actual battle at Roncesvalles, Charlemagne took his army into Spain to overthrow the Muslim rulers and to help Christianize the country. Einhard's *Vita Karoli Magni,* the ninth-century biography of Charlemagne, tells us that when Charlemagne was needed elsewhere he left his Breton warden Hrodlund, our Roland, in charge of the rear guard. Though this force was crushed at Roncesvalles, by 800 Charlemagne was able to create a "Spanish March" and maintain an effective barrier between Muslim Spain and his empire. That year, he came to the aid of Pope Leo III, who was locked in a dispute with another putative pontiff. For his support of Leo III, Charlemagne was crowned Emperor of the Romans at St. Peter's Cathedral on Christmas Day, 800.

Roland's death takes place as a result of two factors: Arab military pressure from outside and disaffection within Frankish society. The difference between the Muslims and the Christians at the outset of the poem is that the Christians have a weak spot within their society—Ganelon, Roland's stepfather, who is a traitor. It is only after Ganelon is arrested that the Franks have a chance of defeating the Muslims. Though Charlemagne loses Roland, who he refers to as his political and military "right hand," our hero Roland deals a blow that not only destroys the enemy but aids in the destruction of the Muslim society. Roland has cut off the right hand of Marsiliun, the Muslim king. A difficult blow for anyone, but for a Muslim, who is prohibited in many social and domestic circumstances from using his left hand, he is in effect being exiled from the community he led.

Perhaps paradoxically, Ganelon's betrayal of Charlemagne and Roland helps to solidify the Frankish community. If a society collapses from both dissatisfied forces within the community and pressures from outside, the *Roland* poet lets us know that ultimately Charlemagne's kingdom is safe. The Muslim force is defeated. Ganelon is subjected to the well-established laws and punishments of the community he had forsaken. We are reassured that Carolingian society has proven to be a match for those internal and external forces committed to its annihilation.

In modern terms we can consider the manuscript evidence of *La Chanson de Roland* after 1099 and the preu d'homme it helped perpetuate as a kind of marketing campaign. It may have functioned as part of the general recruitment for the Second Crusade, which took place most intensively between 1106 and 1107. Though the purported spiritual rewards of crusading, a direct journey to paradise with no stay in purgatory, may have appeared enticing, there were a number of practical concerns that would have given knights, their overlords, and their retinues second thoughts about traveling to the Holy Land. Expense was a paramount concern. To arm his knights and provision them for a three-thousand-mile journey that may have taken well over a year cost the equivalent of six times the king's annual income.[4] The king also needed to be sure that his realm was safe while he was away. So if his fellow monarchs also agreed to accompany him on a Crusade, all the better.

King William II of England and King Philip II of France made a mutual decision to go on the second Crusade. This may help explain why the most complete manuscript that exists today is the one on which W. S. Merwin's translation is based. The manuscript is in the Anglo-Norman dialect spoken by the Norman-French conquerors in England. We can imagine without too much difficulty *La Chanson de Roland* inspiring all Christians—not just French Christians or those of French descent in England but also those Anglo-Norman-speaking Saxon warriors who would have made up the bulk of the foot soldiers.

W. S. Merwin's translation itself stands as another manifestation of Roland's *preu d'homme,* another declaration of the values attributed to Carolingian society. And another form of the magnificent poem that encouraged medieval knights to give their lives in service of a feudal and heroic ideal larger than themselves. Because they had faith that their *preu d'homme* would long outlive them. And it has.

NOTES

1. Rowbotham, John Frederick. *Troubadours and the Courts of Love.* New York: MacMillan, 1895.

2. Ibid.

3. Briffault, Robert S. *The Troubadours.* Bloomington: Indiana University Press, 1965.

4. *The Oxford Illustrated History of the Crusades.* Edited by Jonathan Riley-Smith. New York: Oxford University Press, 1995.

NOTES

Note: *Many of the place names in* The Song of Roland *are not recoverable, hence are not cited.*

I

Mahomet: Muhammad, the prophet and founder of Islam, 570–632 A.D.

Appolin: there is no such figure in Islam (Muslims do not invoke or pray to Appolin or any prophet or saint).

II

pagans: the Arabs were highly unlikely to refer to themselves as "non-Christians," but the *Roland* poet certainly wanted to make clear at the outset of the poem that the Frankish enemies were non-Christian.

III

Aix (also known as Aix-St. Chapelle, now Aachen in western Germany): Charlemagne's principal seat of government. Charlemagne built a palace and academy to which came many of the greatest scholars of the age.

vassal: a formal relationship within the feudal system where a person is granted the use of land in return for homage, fealty, and military service to his overlord.

IV

Michaelmas: a festival celebrated on September 29 in honor of the archangel Michael.

VII

Suatilie: a region in Arabia.

X

hostages: the exchange of hostages for the solidification of a peace treaty was a process well regulated in medieval ecclesiastical and secular law. The belief was that the higher the prestige of the men given as hostages, the more likely the enemy would be to keep to the terms of the treaty.

XI

matins: the first of the seven canonical hours, or specific periods of the day set aside for prayer. For a secular man to hear both mass and matins would be unusual. The poet is probably trying to draw, with bold strokes, a portrait of Charlemagne as a highly religious man.

XII

Gascony: a province in southwestern France.

Reims: a city in northeastern France and the site of the cathedral traditionally used for the coronation of later medieval French kings.

XIV

Naples. . . . Sezilie: perhaps Naples to Seville, places where Charlemagne had undertaken campaigns of contest.

XVII

glove and staff: proofs of identity of the messenger, that he truly represents Charlemagne.

XVIII

by my beard: the symbol of a Frankish man's masculinity.

XXVII

Murglies: it was a long-standing Germanic tradition to give swords names and attribute to them human properties.

Stirrup: the stirrup was not a common part of Carolingian horse equipment. A ninth-century statue of Charlemagne in the Louvre shows him mounted on a horse without stirrups. This technology was borrowed from the East and only become widely used later in the Middle Ages.

XXVIII

Puille: Pulia, a city in southern Italy.

tribute for Saint Peter: also known as "Peter's pence," an annual tax, a penny, from each Christian household, paid to the Papal See. Each nation was responsible for collecting and delivering this tribute to the Pope in Rome.

XXIX

Carcassonne: a walled city in southwestern France. The town did not actually surrender to Charlemagne. The legend at the castle tells that Charlemagne besieged the town for five years until there was no food left within the city walls save one pig. The lady of the castle had the pig thrown over the battlements. Charlemagne withdrew his armies, believing that since the city could afford to be so wasteful with food, he would never be able to take the castle.

XXXV

Caliph: a spiritual leader of Islam claiming succession from Muhammad and rulers of Baghdad until 1258.

XLIV

Sizer: a mountain pass in the Pyrenees.

XLVII

Termagant: a female deity erroneously but popularly believed in the Middle Ages to be worshiped by the Muslims. In medieval morality plays she was portrayed as a violent, overbearing, shrewish character.

LIII

Galne: a city in northern Spain at the foot of the Pyrenees.

LV

Count Roland fixes his pennon: the use of heraldic devices such as pennons and crests began soon after the First Crusade.

LVI

ashen lance: wood from the ash tree was used to make the strongest spears and lances.

LVII

Ardennes: then a great forest, now a region largely in Luxembourg.

LXIV

charger: a horse bred to be used exclusively in battle. A mounted armed knight on his charger was the medieval equivalent of a modern tank.

LXV

Hum: a region now in eastern Germany.

LXVIII

Certeine: region on the French side of the Pyrenees.

LXXI

Barbary: region in north Africa extending from western Egypt to the Atlantic Ocean, including Morocco, Algiers, Tunis and Tripoli.

LXXII

Balasquez: region in southern Spain.

LXXIII

Moraine: region in northern Spain.

LXXVII

Cazmarine: city on the coast of Spain.

Primes: a city and region in Italy.

town of Saint Denis: Saint Denis, the patron saint of France, was sent from Rome to preach to the Gauls and became the first bishop of Paris. Under the persecution of the emperor Valerian he was beheaded in Paris. Legend holds that after his beheading he carried his head twelve miles to the town of St. Denis, where the abbey church now stands.

LXXIX

hauberks . . . three thicknesses of chain mail: Muslim troops usually wore leather armor, though men of prestige were as heavily protected as their European opponents.

Viana: the city of Viana do Castelo, a district now in northwest Portugal.

LXXXIII

In this and the following four *laisses,* collectively called the First Horn scene, Oliver repeatedly tries to persuade Roland to summon aid by blowing his horn, the olifant.

XCII

Montjoy: a later medieval battle cry of the knights of France.

XCIII

hauberk: a long defensive shirt made of tiny links of chain mail.

XCVI

Brigal: a region in southwest Switzerland on the Rhône River.

Satan carries off his soul: according to Christian tradition, since Muslims were not Christians, they descended straight to hell.

C

Bordeaux: city in southwestern France. Knights returning from the first Crusade settled in this region and erected churches with a clear Muslim influence on the architecture.

CIII

horn: here, not the olifant but only a horn used to send signals.

CVII

severs the horse's spine: it was considered dishonorable to injure a man's horse, as later, where the Muslim forces kill Veillantif, Roland's horse.

CXIII

dragon as his device: after the First Crusade Muslim warriors adopted the same sort of shields that the Crusaders used.

Galicia: city on the Dniester River.

CXVI

"*Land of the Fathers*": the Frankish kingdom.

CXVIII

patriarch: the bishop of Jerusalem.

Temple of Solomon: the temple built by the tenth century B.C. King of Israel.

CXXII

Cappadocia: an ancient country in Asia Minor.

CXXVII

Chronicle: an unknown written history of the Franks. Some scholars hypothesize that Turoldus, the purported author of Roland, wrote it.

CXLI

farthing: a medieval form of currency; it was one quarter of a penny.

CXLIII

Carthage, Alfrere, Garmalia and Ethiopia: locations in North Africa and around the Mediterranean Sea.

CLXV

water to Roland: thirst was actually the primary killer of a heavily armed knight in the Middle Ages. For years after Roncesvalles, the phrase "to die like Roland" meant to die of thirst.

CLXVIII

brains . . . ears: some scholars believe that Roland's death was caused by the blast on the oliphant rather than from wounds.

CLXXIII

Saint Peter: one of the Twelve Apostles.

Saint Basil (c. 329–379 A.D.): one of the Greek Church fathers.

Saint Denis: first bishop of Paris, martyred in 270 A.D.

CLXXX

Val Tenebrus: a pass in the Pyrenees.

CXCI

Marbrise and Marbrose: cities along the southern coast of Spain.

CXCII

laurel tree: symbol of heroism and victory, perhaps used here ironically because the Muslims will be defeated twice in the poem.

CCVIII

Laon: city in France northeast of Paris.

CCXX

Bretons: Knights from Brittany. During the historical Charlemagne's lifetime Brittany was, at best, a hostile and unwilling member of the Carolingian Empire. It is highly unlikely that these knights were from Brittany itself. They were, more likely, men who served Charlemagne as wardens and paladins over the native people of Brittany.

CCXXXI

Lycia: a country now in southwest Asia Minor.

CCXXXII

Butentrot: the ancient town of Epirus in northwest Greece.

Micenes: perhaps the ancient region of Mycenae on the northwest coast of Asia Minor.

Blos: city on the Loire in north central France.

Sobres and Sores: perhaps in the region along the banks of the Liri River in Italy.

Nigres: perhaps Nijar in southeastern Spain.

CCXXXIII

Val Fuit: in Old French this could translate as "valley of the retreat."

Solterans and Avars: cities in central France.

Brusse: Brussels.

CCXXXIV

Huns: members of a nomadic and warlike group from Asia.

Leus and Astrimonia: places in eastern Germany.

Argoilles: perhaps the region around the Arges River, a tributary of the Danube, in what is now southern Romania.

Clarbone: city in northern France.

CCXXXVI

Ormalians: perhaps those from Hormoz Iran.

Occian: perhaps those Arabs from the western territories governed by the Muslims.

CCLIII

Outremer: French for "over the sea."

CCLXIV

tonsured: heads shaven.

CCLXVII

Saint Seurin: bishop of Trier, Gaul and Bordeaux, noted for his fervent opposition to variations of Christian doctrine.

CCLXXI

Saint Sylvester's day: December 31. Saint Sylvester was pope from 314 to 335. He defined the articles of the Christian faith.

CCLXXIV

Sorence: perhaps Sorrento in southern Italy.

CCLXXVII

his face is swarthy: the ducal family of Anjou were said to be descended from the dark-haired Melusine, the daughter of the devil. It was from their diabolical parentage that Angevin princes acquired their famed dark coloring and dark ungovernable rages.

CCXCI

Toruldus: the purported author of *Roland.*

GLOSSARY OF NAMES

ACELIN: count of Gascony and adviser to Charlemagne.

AELROTH: Marsiliun's nephew and counselor.

ALDE: Oliver's sister and Roland's fiancée.

ALMACE: Archbishop Turpin's sword.

ALMARIS, KING OF BELFERNE: baron, one of Marsiliun's advisers.

ALPHAIEN, DUKE: Marsiliun's adviser.

ANSEIS: a French baron in Roland's army.

ANTELME OF MAIENCE: a French baron in Charlemagne's army.

ASTOR: a French baron in Roland's army.

AUSTORIE: lord of Valence and Envers-sur-Rhone, knight in Roland's army.

BALASQUEZ, EMIR OF: a handsome soldier in Marsiliun's army.

BALDEWIN: son and heir of Ganelon.

BALIGANT: Marsiliun's overlord.

BASAN: a French messenger.

BASILIE: a French messenger.

BERENGER: a French baron in Roland's army.

BEVUN: baron of Belne and Digun, one of Roland's men.

BLANCANDRIN: Marsiliun's foremost adviser.

BRAMIMONDE: Marsiliun's wife.

CALIPH: Marsiliun's uncle and one of his advisers.

CHARLEMAGNE: Holy Roman Emperor and king of the Franks.

CHERNUBLE: baron, one of Marsiliun's advisers.

CLARIEN: one of King Maltraien's two sons.

CLARIFAN: one of King Maltraien's two sons.

CLARIN OF BALAGUET: baron, one of Marsiliun's advisers.

CLIMORIN: one of Marsiliun's advisers.

CORSALIS, KING: from Barbary, a region in north Africa extending from western Egypt to the Atlantic Ocean.

DAMAPORT, KING: one of the nobles who have come with Baligant from Arabia to help Marsiliun.

DURENDAL: Roland's sword.

ENGELER OF BORDEAUX: French baron.

ENGELER OF GASCONY: French baron.

ESCABABI: baron, one of Marsiliun's advisers.

ESCREMIZ OF VALTERNE: one of Marsiliun's soldiers.

ESPANELIZ: one of King Baligant's followers.

ESPRIERIS: Moorish baron.

ESTAMARIN: baron, one of Marsiliun's advisers.

ESTRAMARIZ: one of Marsiliun's soldiers.

ESTURGANT: one of Marsiliun's soldiers.

EUDROPIN: baron, one of Marsiliun's advisers.

FALDRUN OF PUI: Moorish baron.

FULSARUN: Marsiliun's brother.

GAIGNUN: Marsiliun's horse.

GANELON: French baron, Roland's stepfather, and one of Charlemagne's advisers.

GAULTER OF HUM, COUNT: one of Roland's knights.

GEBOIN: one of Charlemagne's soldiers.

GEFREY OF ANJOU: French baron, brother to the champion Thierry, and one of Charlemagne's advisers.

GEMALFIN: one of the Emir Baligant's favorite soldiers.

GERARD (THE OLD) OF ROUSSILLON: soldier in Roland's army.

GERER, COUNT: one of Charlemagne's advisers, who joins Roland in the rear guard.

GERIN: French baron, one of Charlemagne's advisers, who joins Roland's forces.

GODSELME: French baron.

GRAMMIMUND: Valdebrun's horse.

GRANDONIES: the king of Cappadocia's son.

GUARLAN THE BEARDED: baron, one of Marsiliun's advisers.

GUINEMANS, COUNT: one of Charlemagne's soldiers and part of the Frankish force that rides out against Emir Baligant after the battle at Roncesvalles.

GUINEMER: Ganelon's uncle.

GUIUN OF SAINT ANTHONY: soldier in Roland's army.

HAIMON OF GALICIA: one of Charlemagne's trusted soldiers.

HALTECLERE: Oliver's sword.

HENRY: French baron, nephew of Richard the Elder, and one of Charlemagne's advisers.

HERMAN, DUKE OF TRACE: one of Charlemagne's trusted soldiers.

IVUN: One of Roland's soldiers.

JANGLEU OF OUTREMER: one of Charlemagne's soldiers.

JOUNER: baron, one of Marsiliun's advisers.

JOYEUSE: Charlemagne's sword.

JOZERAN OF PROVENCE: French baron and one of Charlemagne's trusted soldiers.

JURFALEU THE BLOND: Marsiliun's son.

JUSTIN OF VAL FERREE: baron, one of Marsiliun's advisers.

LORANT: one of Charlemagne's soldiers.

MACHINER: baron, one of Marsiliun's advisers.

MAHEU: baron, one of Marsiliun's advisers.

MALDUIT: Marsiliun's treasurer.

MALPALIN OF NARBONNE: a soldier Charlemagne defeated in the battle at Roncesvalles.

MALPRIMIS OF BRIGANT: the son of Emir Baligant and one of Marsliun's soldiers.

MALQUAINT: an African king's son, baron, and one of Marsiliun's advisers.

MALUN: baron, one of Marsiliun's advisers.

MARGANICE: Marsiliun's uncle and Lord of Carthage, Alfrere, Garmalia, and Ethiopia.

MARGARIT, COUNT: baron, one of Marsiliun's advisers.

MARSILIUN: King of the Muslims in Spain.

MILUN, COUNT OF: cousin of Tedbalt of Reims and one of Charlemagne's advisers.

MURGLIES: Ganelon's sword.

NAIMES: Charlemagne's chief and most valued adviser.

NEVELUN, COUNT: one of Charlemagne's advisers.

OEDUN: French baron, one of Charlemagne's advisers.

OGER OF DENMARK, DUKE: one of Charlemagne's advisers.

OLIVER: French baron, part of Roland's forces.

OTUN, MARQUIS: one of Roland's soldiers.

PASSELCERF: Count Gerer's horse.

PINABEL (OF SORENCE): one of Charlemagne's advisers.

PRIAMUN: baron, one of Marsiliun's advisers.

RABEL, COUNT: one of Charlemagne's soldiers and part of the Frankish force that rides out against Emir Baligant after the battle at Roncesvalles.

REMBALT OF GALICIA: one of Charlemagne's trusted soldiers.

RICHARD THE ELDER: French baron and one of Charlemagne's advisers.

ROLAND: French baron and Charlemagne's nephew.

SANSUN, DUKE OF: one of Charlemagne's barons and advisers.

SAUT-PERDUE: Prince Malquaint's horse.

SIGLOREL: a Muslim magician who is taken straight to hell upon his death.

SOREL: Count Gerin's horse.

TACHEBRUN: Ganelon's horse.

TEDBALT OF REIMS: French baron and one of Charlemagne's advisers.

TENDENCUR: one of Charlemagne's horses.

THIERRY, DUKE OF ARGONNE: one of Charlemagne's knights.

TIMOZEL: a soldier in Marsiliun's army.

TORLEU, KING: one of the nobles who have come with Baligant from Arabia to help Marsiliun.

TORULDUS: the purported author of *La Chanson*, he indicates in the last line that he has written it down rather than composed it.

TURGIS OF TURTELUSE: a count in Marsiliun's army.

TURPIN, ARCHBISHOP: French baron, religious adviser to Roland.

VALDEBRUN: Marsiliun's godfather and adviser.

VEILLANTIF: Roland's horse.

VIVIEN, KING: mentioned in the last lines of *La Chanson*, he writes to Charlemagne to ask for help in fighting the forces besieging him at Imphe.

WILLIAM OF BLAYE: one of Charlemagne's advisers.

YVOERIE: soldier in Roland's army.

SELECT BIBLIOGRAPHY

SOURCES IN ENGLISH

Ashe, Laura, "A Prayer and a Warcry: The Creation of a Secular Religion in the *Song of Roland*," *Cambridge Quarterly* 28 (1999): 349–67.

Bliese, John R. E., "Fighting Spirit and Literary Genre: A Comparison of Battle Exhortations in the 'Song of Roland' and in Chronicles of the Central Middle Ages," *Neuphilologische Mitteilungen: Bulletin de la Société Néophilologique* (Bulletin of the Modern Language Society, Helsinki, Finland) 96 (1995): 417–36.

Buchler, Alfred, "Olifan, Graisles, Buisines and Taburs: The Music of War and the Structure and Dating of the Oxford Roland," *Olifant: A Publication of the Société Rencesvals* 17 (1992): 145–67.

Bulatkin, Eleanor Webster. *Structural Arithmetic Metaphor in the Oxford "Roland."* Columbus: Ohio State University Press, 1972.

Cook, Robert Francis. *The Sense of the "Song of Roland."* Ithaca: Cornell University Press, 1987.

Cotton, William T. *"Par amur et par feid:* Keeping Faith and the Varieties of Feudalism in *La Chanson de Roland."* In *The Rusted Hauberk: Feudal Ideals of Order and Their Decline,* edited by Liam O. Purdon and Cindy L. Vitto. Gainesville: University Press of Florida, 1994.

Duggan, Joseph J. *The Song of Roland: Formulaic Style and Poetic Craft.* Berkeley: University of California Press, 1973.

Earnhart, Brady, "Hero as Author in The Song of Roland," *Olifant: A Publication of the Société Rencesvals* 18 (1993): 84–93.

Goldin, Frederick, "Mickel's Ganelon, Treason and the 'Chanson de Roland,' " *Olifant: A Publication of the Société Rencesvals* 17 (1992): 196–212.

Haidu, Peter. *The Subject of Violence: The Song of Roland and the Birth of the State.* Bloomington: Indiana University Press, 1993.

Hindley, Alan, and Brian J. Levy. *The Old French Epic: Texts, Commentaries, Notes.* Louvain (Belgium): Peeters, 1983.

Irving, Edward B. "Heroic Role-Models: Beowulf and Others." In *Heroic Po-*

etry in the Anglo-Saxon Period: Studies in Honor of Jess B. Bessinger, Jr., edited by Helen Damico and John Leyerle. Kalamazoo, Mich.: Medieval Institute Publications, 1993.

Jones, George Fenwick. *The Ethos of the Song of Roland.* Baltimore: Johns Hopkins Press, 1963.

Kibler, William W. "The Prologue to the Lyon Manuscript of the *Chanson de Roland.*" In *Continuations: Essays on Medieval French Literature and Language in Honor of John L. Grigsby,* edited by Norris J. Lacy and Gloria Torrini-Roblin. Birmingham, Ala.: Summa, 1989.

Lejeune, Rita, and Jacques Stiennon. *The Legend of Roland in the Middle Ages.* New York: Phaidon, 1971.

Masters, Bernadette A. "The Oxford Roland as an Ahistorical Document: A Tale of Ghosts or a Ghost of a Tale?" In *The Epic in History,* edited by Lola Sharon Davidson, S. N. Mukherjee, and Z. Zlatar. Sydney (Australia): Sydney Association for Studies in Society and Culture, 1994.

Morris, Matthew W., "The 'Other' as a Reflection of Augustinism in the *Chanson de Roland, Medieval Perspectives* 14 (1999): 166–76.

Nichols, Stephen G. *Formulaic Diction and Thematic Composition in the Chanson de Roland.* Chapel Hill: University of North Carolina Press, 1961.

Owen, D. D. R. *The Legend of Roland: A Pageant of the Middle Ages.* London: Phaidon, 1973.

Pei, Mario. *French Precursors of the Chanson de Roland.* New York: Columbia University Press, 1948.

Reisinger, Deborah Streifford, "The Other and the Same: The Ambiguous Role of the Saracen in *La chanson de Roland,*" *RLA: Romance Languages Annual* 9 (1997): 94–97.

Rickel, Emanuel J. "*Judicium Dei* and the Structure of *La Chanson de Roland.*" In *Studies in Honor of Hans-Erich Keller: Medieval French and Occitan Literature and Romance Linguistics,* edited by Rupert T. Pickens. Kalamazoo, Mich.: Medieval Institute Publications, 1993.

Shepherd, Stephen H. A., " 'I Haue Gone for Thi Sak Wonderfull Wais': The Middle English Fragment of *The Song of Roland.*" *Olifant: A Publication of the Société Rencesvals* 11 (1986): 219–36.

Terry, Patricia, "Roland at Roncevaux: A Vote for the Angels," *Olifant: A Publication of the Société Rencesvals* 14 (1989): 155–64.

Vance, Eugene. *Reading the Song of Roland.* Englewood Cliffs, N.J., Prentice-Hall, 1970.

———, "Style and Value: From Soldier to Pilgrim in the *Song of Roland,*" *Yale French Studies* (1991): 75–96.

SOURCES IN FRENCH

Bellon, Roger. *Linguistique médiévale. L'épreuve d'ancien français aux concours.* Paris: Armand Colin, 1995.

Cook, Robert. "*La Mort exemplaire de Gautier del Hum.*" In *Et c'est la fin pour quoi sommes ensemble: Hommage à Jean Dufourne: littérature, histoire et langue du moyen âge,* edited by Jean-Claude Aubailly. Paris: Champion, 1993.

Diament, Henri, "Deux toponymes mysterieux de la Chanson de Roland: Seinz et Besencun, clefs pour la sémantique territoriale du mot France au XIe siècle." In *De l'aventure épique à l'aventure romanesque: Mélanges offerts à André de Mandach par ses amis, collegues et élevès,* edited by Jacques Chocheyras. Bern (Switzerland): Peter Lang, 1997.

Dickman, Adolphe Jacques. *Le rôle du surnaturel dans les chansons de geste.* Iowa City: State University of Iowa, 1925.

Duggan, Joseph J. "*L'Episode d'Aude dans la tradition en rime de la Chanson de Roland.*" In *Charlemagne in the North: Proceedings of the 12th International Conference of the Société Roncesvals,* Edinburgh, 4–11 August 1991, edited by Philip E. Bennett, Anne Elizabeth Cobby, and Graham A. Runnalls. Edinburgh: Société Rencesvals British Branch, 1993.

Faucon, Jean-Claude. "*La Bataille (du poeme) de Roncevaux ou l'exquise aménité des médiévistes du XIXe siècle.*" In *Chemins ouverts: Mélanges offerts à Claude Sicard,* edited by Sylvie Vignes. Toulouse (France): Les Presses Universitaires du Mirail, 1998.

Lecouteux, Claude. *Au-delà du merveilleux: Essai sur les mentalités du moyen âge,* 2nd edition. Paris: Presses de l'Université de Paris-Sorbonne, 1998.

Magnusdottir, Asdis R. "*Le Meilleur Cor du monde: L'Olifant dans la cinquième branche de la Saga de Karlamagnus.*" *Recherches et Travaux* 9 (1998): 55–62.

Mireaux, Emile. *La Chanson de Roland et l'historie de France.* Paris: A. Michel, 1943.

Morrissey, Robert J. *L'empereur à la barbe fleurie: Charlemagne dans la mythologie et l'histoire de France.* Paris: Gallimard, 1997.

Paris, Gaston Bruno Paulin. *Légendes du moyen âge.* Paris: Hachette et cie, 1908.

Pensom, Roger. "*Histoire et poesie dans la Chanson de Roland.*" *Romania: Revue Consacrée à l'Étude des Langues et des Littératures Romanes* 113 (1992–1995): 373–82.

Stanesco, Michel. *Lire le moyen âge.* Paris: Dunod, 1998.

Vos, Marianne Cramer. "*La Mort soudaine d'Aude, icone feminine, dans le Roland d'Oxford.*" In *Charlemagne in the North: Proceedings of the 12th International Conference of the Société Roncesvals,* Edinburgh, 4–11 August 1991, edited by Philip E. Bennett, Anne Elizabeth Cobby, and Graham A. Runnalls. Edinburgh: Société Rencesvals British Branch, 1993.

MODERN LIBRARY IS ONLINE AT
WWW.MODERNLIBRARY.COM

MODERN LIBRARY ONLINE IS YOUR GUIDE
TO CLASSIC LITERATURE ON THE WEB

THE MODERN LIBRARY E-NEWSLETTER

Our free e-mail newsletter is sent to subscribers, and features sample chapters, interviews with and essays by our authors, upcoming books, special promotions, announcements, and news.

To subscribe to the Modern Library e-newsletter, send a blank e-mail to: **sub_modernlibrary@info.randomhouse.com** or visit **www.modernlibrary.com**

THE MODERN LIBRARY WEBSITE

Check out the Modern Library website at
www.modernlibrary.com for:

- The Modern Library e-newsletter
- A list of our current and upcoming titles and series
- Reading Group Guides and exclusive author spotlights
- Special features with information on the classics and other paperback series
- Excerpts from new releases and other titles
- A list of our e-books and information on where to buy them
- The Modern Library Editorial Board's 100 Best Novels and 100 Best Nonfiction Books of the Twentieth Century written in the English language
- News and announcements

Questions? E-mail us at **modernlibrary@randomhouse.com**.
For questions about examination or desk copies, please visit
the Random House Academic Resources site at
www.randomhouse.com/academic